I0622036

Dedication

To my partner Alison Hepburn for her love, support and
patient early reads, and our daughter Katy.
I will be forever delighted by their genuine surprise
when I told them I was writing this book.

Also to my good friend and business partner Jacky Fitt
for her early read and encouragement.

Finally to Marcus Parry for his encyclopedic knowledge of
commas, semicolons, colons and en dashes, and knowing
when to use them.

I couldn't have done it without you all.

Chapter 1

The early morning sun cast a golden glow over the streets of Exeter, bathing the historic Cathedral Green in a soft, warm light. It was one of those perfect late summer days where the sky was a vivid blue, unmarred by a single cloud; a light breeze carried the scent of freshly cut grass from the Green. Edward Voss, proprietor of Voss Antiquarian Books, stood at the door of his modest yet elegant shop, momentarily pausing to take in the tranquillity of the scene before him.

His shop, nestled between a centuries-old tearoom and a boutique selling artisanal crafts, was a small but distinguished establishment. The window display, carefully curated by Edward himself, featured a selection of rare and valuable books, some leather-bound volumes with gold leaf embossing, others original manuscripts by long-forgotten authors. To the casual passerby, the shop might appear quaint, but to the discerning collector, it was a treasure trove of historical knowledge and literary artefacts.

Edward had opened his shop nearly a decade ago after leaving the University. He had always loved history, and this had led him to a lifelong fascination with rare books and manuscripts. On graduation, he had briefly worked as an assistant to Dr Evelyn Merton, but that finished at the end of the summer term ten years ago. When the opportunity to open a shop on Cathedral Green had presented itself, he seized it as a way to marry his love for history with the freedom of running his own business. It meant he could show his new wife, Victoria, that he could be somebody, although he had no intention of building the bookshop empire she would have undoubtedly preferred.

Victoria had always been the family rebel, kicking against the strictures that confined her as the only daughter of the Berger family. Her brothers had always been allowed so much more freedom, and this injustice fuelled her rebellion. She had thrown herself at Edward, who she knew would be seen as unacceptable to her father. Her outrageous flirting had taken Edward unawares; he felt honoured to have all this attention lavished upon him by this young, beautiful society woman. He fell deeply in love with her; he felt that he had to create his place in the family to make Victoria and the rest of them respect him. They had a whirlwind courtship, which led quickly to marriage, and then everything seemed to change. He thought he had loved Victoria but had never really understood her, or indeed, she him. Once they were married, she found that her rebellion had not given her what she wanted; quite the opposite, and she had quickly come to despise Edward almost as much as the rest of her family had done from the very start of their romance.

Today, as on most days, he began his morning with a routine that had become second nature. He reached into the inner pocket of his tweed jacket and retrieved an old-fashioned brass key. With a satisfying click, the heavy oak door unlocked, and he stepped inside. The familiar smell of aged paper, leather and wood greeted him, a scent that always felt like a welcome home.

The inside of the shop was dimly lit, with only a few slivers of sunlight filtering through the blinds that had been drawn the night before. The space was cosy in a cluttered but organised way, tall, dark wooden bookshelves lining the walls from floor to ceiling, each one filled with volumes dating back centuries. A few freestanding bookshelves stood in the middle of the room, and towards the back of the shop was a small reading area, complete with a worn leather armchair and an antique lamp. He smiled to himself – so much better than the chain bookshops.

Edward turned on the small desk lamp that illuminated his worktable, full of books waiting to be catalogued, handwritten invoices and his notebook, a journal filled with his musings, records and the occasional sketch. He took a deep breath, enjoying the quiet serenity of the shop before the day officially began. He made his usual tea in his porcelain teapot, placed the tea cosy on the pot and positioned it on his desk in its special spot away from any important books while he waited for the tea to brew.

The first order of business was to check on the inventory, something he did every morning. He walked the length of the shelves, running his fingers along the spines of the books, checking for any that might need attention or repair. Each book held a story, not just in its contents, but in its journey through time, who had owned it, where it had travelled, and how it had survived the passage of centuries. For him, this was the magic of antiquarian books, and he never tired of it.

As he finished his morning rounds, Edward glanced at the clock. It was nearly time to open the shop. He walked back to the door and flipped the old cardboard sign from "Closed" to "Open" and opened the blinds, letting in the light. He propped the door slightly ajar, a subtle invitation to anyone who might be passing by. Edward preferred this more casual approach, never one for aggressive sales tactics, to him, they never felt quite right. He believed that if someone was truly interested in the world of rare books, they would find their way to him.

As the day progressed, the usual rhythm of the business day began. A few regular customers dropped by an elderly professor from the university who was searching for an elusive edition of a 19th-century travel journal; a local historian who often spent hours in the reading corner, poring over medieval manuscripts. Edward greeted each one with a polite nod and understated warmth, always happy to assist in their search for knowledge or to simply engage in a quiet conversation about their latest findings. Every day, he hoped Evelyn would come to the shop, but she never did, although the hope never diminished.

Around midday, a couple entered the shop, drawn in by the window display. Edward immediately recognised them as tourists, their curious eyes scanning the shelves with a mix of awe and uncertainty. He knew by experience that they were not the type to buy anything, but Edward welcomed them with the same attentiveness as he did his more frequent visitors. He watched as they hesitated in front of an ornately bound edition of *Paradise Lost*. The man picked it up, admiring the gold leaf on the cover, but quickly replaced it after glancing at the price tag. Edward chuckled to himself but offered no comment. He knew better than to press; books like this sold themselves only to those who truly understood their value.

After the couple left, Edward took a moment to stretch and enjoy a brief respite. He walked to the front of the shop and stepped outside, standing beneath the shade of a nearby tree. The Cathedral bells tolled, the sound reverberating around the Green. He smiled, thinking about how lucky he was to work in such a picturesque location. It wasn't the bustling world of academia, nor the competitive environment of business, that had attracted him to this life, but the quiet dignity of the acquisition of knowledge.

As he stood outside, he noticed a familiar face across the Green, Victoria deep in conversation with her younger brother, Thomas, their sharp features and aura of entitlement making them unmistakably members of the Berger family. His relationship with Victoria, he thought, had started with shared interests in history. However, her historical interest had been as short-lived as their courtship, and after the wedding, she seemed to become bored with history and him. Love and passion had not lasted beyond the wedding day, and fairly quickly, the cracks had begun to show. At first, Victoria had not known about Edward's admiration of his former boss, and when she found out, it became a constant source of tension between them and was now noticeable, even in public. Edward now felt trapped in his marriage and diminished by the disapproval of Victoria's family; the lonelier he felt, the more he hankered for the days working for Evelyn.

Edward watched as Victoria and Thomas disappeared from view, feeling his rage rising. He returned inside the shop, his mood now darker. The shop, once a sanctuary, felt a bit more suffocating in that moment. He knew with this anger and resentment, he was walking a dangerous path, and yet, he couldn't help himself.

Shaking off these thoughts, Edward returned to his work. A box of newly acquired books awaited his attention, and he lost himself in cataloguing them. This was the part of the job he loved the most, the discovery of new (or old) treasures, each book a doorway into another time, another life. He examined each volume, checking its condition, recording its provenance, and deciding where he should place it in the shop.

As the afternoon wore on, more customers came and went. Some bought books, others left empty-handed, hopefully enriched by their experience. As the sun began to cast long shadows across the Green, Edward prepared to close up for the day. He lowered the blinds and locked the front door, sealing the shop in its familiar cocoon of quiet. He washed his cup and teapot and left them to dry overnight, ready for the next day.

Before leaving, Edward lingered by the reading corner, where an ancient manuscript lay open on the table. It was a Latin text from the 14th century, a work he had been studying in his spare time. He traced the faded ink with his fingertip, feeling a deep connection to the past and to the scholars and scribes who had created this very book many centuries before. For Edward, this was the true magic of his work, connecting with history in a way that few others could.

When Edward left the shop, stepping out into the cool early evening air, it had started to drizzle slightly. The city was quieter now, the daytime crowds thinning as the shops and cafés closed for the night. He took one last look at his shop, feeling a sense of pride; as he walked away, the bells of Exeter Cathedral rang once more, their sonorous chimes a reminder that, like the books he cherished, some things endured through the ages.

Chapter 2

Dr Evelyn Merton was taking a rare day off at home from her research. It was a sunny day, and the students were still off on their summer break, and, while the world of research never really stops, she had told herself that she did need to take time away from her office to think. Evelyn now works at Exeter University after a glittering academic rise in her field of medieval history after gaining her PhD at Balliol College, Oxford.

During her early years at Exeter University, she had lived in a flat on campus, a short walk from her department. She was recognised by students and staff, and she felt, for the first time in her life, part of a community. She even had a few people whom she considered friends rather than just colleagues. She taught students, and the most gifted she encouraged to help in her research.

As she deadheaded some flowers, he chatted to her cat, who was dozing in the borders in the shade with not the slightest intention of doing anything useful. That was what she loved about them, content and not driven, something to aspire to. Her thoughts drifted to her current assistant, Miranda Jackson – she reminded Evelyn of herself at that age. Miranda was very talented, but unlike Evelyn, also quite gregarious and socially aware, two things that Evelyn had never achieved. Miranda was her first assistant for about ten years, and she admired her for her intellect and, at the same time, felt comfortable in her company. Miranda had grown up near Exeter and spoke with a soft Devon burr. She was tall and had her unique style developed from hours rooting through the charity shops in the city and balancing her finds with a few very well-chosen accessories and always good boots. Her long, wavy brown hair was always loose and gave the impression it was trying to escape from under the beanie she usually wore when summer had finished.

Evelyn often scolded herself for her lack of engagement with the modern world when she was engrossed in research, and this, over the years, had led to some quite embarrassing misunderstandings. These days, Evelyn occasionally found herself thinking about what Miranda would do. How things had changed in the last three months.

Her thoughts now turned back to her last assistant ten years earlier. Edward Voss, her assistant at the time, had been an altogether different character from Miranda. He had started to make her feel very uncomfortable, but she could never quite work out why. As two introverts, their conversations were always short, to the point and restricted to their work. Edward kept himself very much to himself, was punctual and had obsessive habits built up around his schedule, the arrangement of his desk and hated it if anyone ever called him Ed. He seemed content to operate in her orbit, but that had begun to change.

It started with her catching him just staring at her across the office, and if she caught his eye, he would start shuffling papers around his desk for no reason, a little like a cat washing itself when caught out. Then his work seemed to become less focused, and there were the glaring errors, something Evelyn would not tolerate. To start off with, the errors could have been seen as simple slips, but they got worse and moved towards unsubstantiated claims and then to lies. He was researching on her behalf, and she found herself having to check on his work rather than rely on it. If she missed something and it got published, it could irreparably damage her reputation. Something had to be done.

Evelyn shuddered as she remembered the day of Edward's annual review interview, and she had not been looking forward to it. She had a feeling that she was going to have to find a new, more reliable researcher. At first, Edward's mistakes had been rare; they were now coming in waves, and it was beginning to impact on her ability to carry on her research. Edward had come into the interview, and the atmosphere was very, very tense. The interview started with the usual social pleasantries, good practice to help the interviewee relax; however, he didn't. Evelyn asked about Edward's work and its general decline. His body language, never relaxed, became even more awkward and closed as she listed some of the most recent errors. When she looked up, she could see he was blushing; Evelyn felt very vulnerable, and Edward's presence in the small office suddenly felt very oppressive.

Then Edward's dam of emotions broke, and he shouted at her about how aloof she was, how he never felt respected, how difficult she was both as a senior academic and as a human being. Just who was being reviewed? How dare he! Then, out of the blue, a tirade about his undying love for her, how he worshipped her and how he wanted them to leave the University to live together, perhaps even emigrate to a distant land to start a new life. Evelyn had to get out of that room; she did not know what to do other than she never wanted to be in the same room with this man again, let alone work with him. She left, leaving him sitting in the chair, rage still making his heart pound.

Evelyn had rushed to see her friend Jill in HR to explain what had happened and how she felt she had to terminate Edward's association with her work and to warn her of his apparent mania and instability. Jill understood and said she would deal with the situation. Within days, Edward had received a termination letter, which he felt was like a dagger to his heart; he was never seen in Evelyn's department again. This, however, was only the beginning. Evelyn started getting occasional passive-aggressive letters, left on her desk overnight, with no indication who had left them and not traceable because they were printed. These became more deeply unsettling as the frequency increased. To start with, she threw them away, thinking they were pranks. However, as more notes appeared, they spread under the windscreen wipers of her car and then the most sinister under the door of her flat.

After this, she had felt compelled to move out of her beloved flat on campus. These days, she had a long bus ride to work, and this felt more like traditional commuting; it made her feel disconnected from University life. Evelyn now lived alone in a quaint, Tudor cottage in the village of Pinhoe, just outside Exeter. Although she loved it, she still hankered after her campus flat and the community she felt she had been compelled to leave.

Over the years, she had made the cottage very much her own home, her retreat from academia. It was nestled in a dip at the edge of the village, surrounded by a small garden filled with herbs and flowers. Despite her professional acclaim, Evelyn was a private person; her reputation in the village was that she was kind but somewhat reclusive. Such was her fear of the letters starting again, she had been very careful to ensure only very few colleagues knew her address, and when she shared it, she also emphasised how it must remain secret. These days, her closest companions were her two cats, Merlin and Morgana, who were often seen lounging in her garden, where their only inconvenience was having to move to a new shady spot when the sun moved around.

As the sun began to sink over the horizon and a drizzle filled the air, Evelyn decided to go indoors and settle into an evening planning her week with Miranda. They had recently taken to meeting up on a Sunday evening; to start with, it was all about planning the week's work, now it had grown into more of a friendship with a little organisation if they had to, but that was not always on the agenda.

Chapter 3

Before Edward started his walk home, he took a moment to marvel at the grandeur of Exeter Cathedral, its ancient stones starting to turn a murky grey in the evening drizzle. His mind was elsewhere, clouded with the dark thoughts about his home life that had plagued him for years. His step was heavier than it had been on his way in this morning, tension building with every step closer to home. This was not the sign of a good marriage, and Edward knew it, but what could he do about it?

He began his walk home, down the narrow path towards the High Street and headed down towards Sidwell Street, his heart growing heavier with each step. The High Street's hustle and bustle of the shoppers had morphed into the night-time revellers and partygoers. Edward was aching for a quiet evening, but there was no peace for him; his life, once full of promise and intellectual excitement, had turned into something unrecognisable, a life dominated by resentment, unfulfilled dreams, and a simmering anger that he could no longer control.

As he walked, Edward's thoughts drifted back to what might have been. He had been a rising star in the field of medieval history, but somewhere along the way, his dreams had slipped away, and his life had taken a direction he had never intended. In his mind, it had all started with Victoria. Meeting her had seemed like the beginning of something extraordinary: she was beautiful, confident, and came from one of Exeter's most influential families. Marrying her had initially opened doors for Edward, giving him access to circles of power and prestige of which he could have only dreamed.

The reality of his life with Victoria had now become far removed from the fairy tale he had envisioned. The Bergers had expectations, expectations that Edward could never meet. Leonard Berger, Victoria's father, was an archetypal patriarch; he controlled the whole family with a blend of coercion and money. Victoria was strong-willed and stubborn, determined to maintain her independence and the Berger name, something that had stung Edward's pride from the very beginning. The very first example of this was when Leonard bought his daughter a large Victorian townhouse at the top end of Pennsylvania Road when they married, so they were mortgage-free. However, the house was only in Victoria's name, and that snub hurt Edward's pride, and this resentment returned every time he turned the key in the front door. He was always the outsider, the one who had married into the family rather than being born into it. He was barely tolerated, his intellect ignored, and he had never really been accepted by Victoria or her family.

His relationship with Victoria had become a source of constant frustration and, at times, a battleground. He had never been able to shake the feeling that he was an out-of-fashion accessory in her life, someone to be wheeled out at society events but otherwise best ignored. He resented the way Victoria and her family seemed to dominate their marriage, how she or her father were always in control, always making the decisions. He resented her family, with their wealth and power, their ability to move through life without the struggles he had faced. Most of all, he resented himself for what he had become, for the compromises he had made, for the life he had allowed himself to live.

He turned left at the crossroads and then turned into

Longbrook Street, the smell from the chip shop hanging in the air. Edward's thoughts turned to Evelyn Merton. Edward's admiration of her had turned to resentment. Had she valued his work as her assistant? Had she even been aware of his work and dedication? Had she been behind his dismissal from the University History department? Had this driven him into the arms of Victoria and the Berger clan?

Edward was now walking up the hill of Pennsylvania Road, past the Co-op and turning into Powderham Crescent, and then the house came into view. It was a grand house, perched on the hill overlooking the city and, in the other direction, towards the edge of the University campus, a constant reminder of what could have been. The imposing façade of the four-storey Victorian house, with its tall windows and intricate stonework, was a symbol of the Berger family's status. He also felt that by living in this house, they were controlled by an obligation to "the family." To Edward, it was a prison, Victoria's house with him a mere inmate, a place where his dreams had withered and died and his sense of injustice had flourished.

As he walked up the path to the front door, his heart sank. The house was beautiful, yes, but it was not his. He could feel the day's frustrations bearing down on him. He pushed open the door and stepped inside. The interior of the house was as grand as the exterior, with high ceilings and elegant furnishings. The entrance hall was growing dark, the cold, ornate Victorian tiled floor was less than welcoming, and stairs lined with portraits of the Berger family made him feel more like he was a visitor to a National Trust house rather than coming home.

Victoria looked up as he came in, her expression cool and composed as she reclined on a chaise longue, a glass of sparkling wine in her hand. She was dressed impeccably, as she always was, in a designer dress that spoke of wealth and sophistication. "You're late," she said, her tone neutral but with an edge that Edward had come to recognise all too well.

"I had to close up the shop and sort out a new delivery of books," Edward replied, trying to keep his voice steady. He could feel the tension building, the rage that had been simmering all day threatened to spill over.

Victoria took a sip of wine, her eyes never leaving his. "The shop. That little hobby of yours. I don't understand why you insist on spending so much time there. You could be doing so much more, Edward. You're wasting your potential. No one is interested in old books these days."

It was a familiar refrain, one that Edward had heard countless times before. Victoria had never understood his love for antiquarian books, for the quiet, scholarly life he had once dreamed of. To her, it was a waste, a sign that he wasn't living up to the expectations that came with being part of the Berger family; he wasn't building an empire at all.

"I enjoy it," Edward said, his voice tight. "It's what I love."

Victoria's expression hardened. "Love? Edward, you're better than that. You could be doing something important, something meaningful. Instead, you're hiding away in that dusty old shop, surrounded by relics of the past"

"Relics of the past?" Edward's voice rose, the anger that had been building all day finally breaking free. "Is that how you see it? Is that how you see me?"

Victoria's eyes narrowed. "You know that's not what I meant. But you're wasting your talents. You could be making a real impact, but instead, you're stuck in that one shop, clinging to some outdated notion of who you are. The world has moved on, so should you."

"And what would you have me do, Victoria?" Edward's voice was cold now, his anger giving way to a deep, bitter resentment. "Be more like you? Like your family? I'm not a Berger, Victoria. I'll never be a Berger. I'm just the man you happened to marry, the man who will never be good enough for you or your family."

Victoria stared at him, her expression unreadable. "Edward, that's not fair."

"Isn't it?" Edward shot back. "You've never accepted me for who I am. You've always wanted me to be something I'm not. Well, I'm tired, Victoria. I'm tired of pretending, of trying to live up to your impossible standards. I'm tired of this life."

For a moment, there was silence. The tension seemed to crackle in the air, a palpable force that threatened to tear them apart.

Victoria finally broke the silence. "If you're so unhappy, Edward, then why do you stay?"

The question hung in the air, and Edward found himself at a loss for words. Why did he stay? Was it out of love? Obligation? Fear of the unknown? Or was it simply because he didn't know how to leave, didn't know how to walk away from this life, even if it was a life that brought him nothing but pain?

"I don't know," he said finally, his voice barely above a whisper. "I just don't know why I stay."

Victoria sighed, the tension in her shoulders easing slightly. "Edward, I never wanted you to feel like this. But you have to understand, this is the life we chose. We committed, and we have to make it work."

"But at what cost, Victoria?" Edward's voice was filled with bitterness. "At what cost?"

Victoria didn't answer, and the silence between them grew heavier, filled with the unspoken words and unresolved conflicts.

Edward turned away, unable to bear the sight of her cool, composed look any longer. He walked to the window. The sun had now completely disappeared, and he stared out into the early autumnal darkness, his mind racing with thoughts of what could have been. He could have had a different life, a life filled with the passion for history that had once consumed him, a life free from the suffocating expectations of the Berger family. He could have been someone else, someone happier, someone who didn't feel like a stranger in his own home. But those dreams were gone now, buried under the years of bitterness. He stood, staring out into the night, the streetlights casting strange shadows across the all too familiar street; the darkness outside seemed to match his dark mood that he feared would consume him entirely if he didn't find a way to escape it. The argument with Victoria had drained him, leaving him feeling hollow and defeated. He didn't know if he had the strength to keep fighting, to keep pretending that everything was okay.

He finally turned away from the window and left the room and made his way to his cold, lonely bedroom at the top of the house: Victoria had decided they should have separate rooms very early on in the marriage. Edward felt a deep sense of despair setting in; the night stretched out before him, and he knew that sleep would bring no respite. His thoughts continued to race, his mind continued to churn, and the resentment that had become a part of him would continue to fester.

As he lay down, he couldn't help but wonder if this was all there was, if this was the life he was destined to live. Something was going to have to change.

Chapter 4

The friendship between Lydia Jones, the wife of Detective Inspector Whipton Barton and Dr Evelyn Merton was an unlikely one. It had developed gradually, built on the kind of trust that can only come from genuine understanding and appreciation of one another's differences.

Lydia had always been a woman of quiet intellect. She was an amateur researcher with a particular interest in the medieval history of Exeter. In complete contrast to Barton, her days were often spent in the archives of the University of Exeter deciphering the stories of the past and unravelling mysteries of a completely different kind. She had first met Evelyn at a conference. Lydia had been somewhat starstruck seeing her; she was a fan of Evelyn's book *Invisible Women: Gender and Power in Medieval England* and wanted to introduce herself to talk about the book. Evelyn's research was groundbreaking, her publications widely respected, and her lectures well attended. What could she, Lydia, say to such an academic? Lydia plucked up her courage and introduced herself, and said how much she admired the book. Despite her success, Evelyn wasn't usually one to engage in idle chatter or superficial relationships; however, she instantly warmed to Lydia's directness, and straightaway they seemed at ease in each other's company. What had begun as a simple inquiry soon evolved into a deeper conversation, and they agreed to meet up again the following week, which was a surprise to them both.

When they met in one of the campus cafés, Evelyn was intrigued by Lydia's knowledge and passion for the subject; she found herself talking at length about the intricacies of medieval Exeter, the very topic that had brought them together. For Lydia, meeting Evelyn was like discovering a kindred spirit. Though they were different in many ways, Evelyn's reserved character and Lydia's quiet curiosity complemented each other, creating a dynamic where both felt understood and appreciated. Both women were fascinated by the past, but their approaches to history were very different, reflecting their personalities. Evelyn approached history with a critical eye, always seeking to challenge established narratives and uncover hidden truths. Lydia, on the other hand, was drawn to the human stories. For her, history was not just a series of dates and facts, but a tapestry of lives, emotions, and a glimpse into another era of experiences. She sought to understand the motivations, fears, and dreams of the people who had lived centuries before, and she often found herself lost in the personal letters and diaries that brought the past to life.

These differences led to many lively discussions. Evelyn would challenge Lydia's interpretations, pushing her to think more critically, while Lydia would encourage Evelyn to consider the emotional and personal aspects of history. While both were quite stubborn, they were prepared to let the other put their point of view without argument or rancour.

Beyond history, they also shared a love for the quiet beauty of the Devon countryside. One of the pivotal moments in their friendship came when Evelyn first invited Lydia to her cottage in Pinhoe. This invitation into her home was a significant gesture of trust, one that marked a deepening of their friendship.

Lydia was taken aback and quite mystified by Evelyn's insistence that she keep the address very much to herself.

This immediately intrigued Lydia, but she did not press for a reason, as she suspected that this was a story that she would one day understand. For Evelyn, inviting Lydia to Pinhoe was not just a social gesture; she was letting Lydia into her private world. Lydia was immediately enchanted by the cottage. It was a magical place, somewhere where the past seemed to come alive.

During her visits, Lydia and Evelyn would spend hours discussing each other's research, sometimes exploring the surrounding countryside, or simply enjoying the peace together. These moments were a respite from the demands of their busy lives, a time to relax and recharge. Over time, Evelyn began to rely on Lydia more and more. She valued her opinion and often sought her advice on both professional and personal matters. Lydia became one of the few people Evelyn would confide in, someone she knew she could trust with her deepest thoughts and concerns.

Lydia was warm and approachable, with a gentle manner that put people at ease. She was a good listener, always willing to lend an ear to those who needed it, and she had a way of making others feel valued and understood. Her kindness and empathy made her well-liked by those who knew her, and she often found herself playing the role of confidante and advisor.

Evelyn, by contrast, was more reserved: to many, she appeared aloof, even intimidating, with her no-nonsense attitude. Beneath this exterior, she was a woman who valued loyalty and integrity above all else. Lydia's warmth and openness gradually broke through Evelyn's reserve, allowing their friendship to grow. Evelyn, who was not used to letting people into her life, found herself trusting Lydia in a way she hadn't trusted anyone in years. She appreciated Lydia's non-judgmental nature, knowing that she could confide in her without fear of being misunderstood or criticised.

Lydia, for her part, saw in Evelyn a woman who had carved out a successful career in a male-dominated field, who had faced numerous challenges but had never wavered in her commitment. Evelyn's determination and confidence inspired Lydia, pushing her to pursue her own goals with greater conviction.

There was something about Lydia's quiet strength and genuine interest in her that made Evelyn feel comfortable, even safe. With Lydia, she felt comfortable asking for advice or opinion. One afternoon, as they sat in the garden of the cottage sipping tea, Evelyn asked if she knew of anyone she could employ as her new assistant in the department.

"I very much value your opinion. I am afraid I am not a very good judge of character, and I have made some terrible mistakes in the past"

Lydia thought this was very unlike Evelyn to express doubt in her judgment.

"You are just so good at reading people," Evelyn continued.

"The name that immediately comes to mind is Miranda Jackson," said Lydia.

Miranda and Lydia had met in one of the archives when they had both applied to review the same document on the same afternoon. They had fallen into conversation about their respective research and realised their interests overlapped more than just this one document. Lydia reminded Miranda of her mother and felt very at ease in her company. Lydia felt at once a glow of satisfaction and surprise that this striking and quite remarkable young woman would be interested in what she was doing. In turn, Miranda had also been curious about Lydia, whose reputation as the wife of DI Barton and as a respected amateur researcher in her own right was widely respected at the University. As often happened with Lydia, a chance meeting had turned into friendship.

At first, Evelyn was characteristically cautious about Lydia's suggestion, but became more intrigued as Lydia positively bubbled with enthusiasm about her new young friend and reluctantly agreed to her bringing Miranda to the cottage. Evelyn didn't want anyone at the University to know she was looking for a new assistant; she would be inundated with application emails, and she didn't have time or patience for that, but more importantly, she trusted Lydia's judgment. She, once again, repeated to Lydia the importance of confidentiality about her home address and requested that she explain this to Miranda.

Chapter 5

Summer was beginning to fade into autumn, and the rain now came rolling from the hills as Lydia and Miranda made their way up the narrow lane leading to Evelyn Merton's secluded cottage. For Lydia, this journey was a familiar one, a comforting ritual in her friendship with Evelyn. For Miranda, it felt like a momentous occasion, her first meeting – or was it an interview – with a renowned historian, a woman whose work she admired, who she hoped might want her to employ her. Miranda was acutely aware of the opportunity that was in front of her. There was also something intriguing about this whole secrecy thing.

As they approached the ivy-covered stone cottage, Miranda felt a flutter of nerves. The cottage appeared to be from another era, a place where history was not just studied but lived. Miranda couldn't help but be impressed by the setting; it was exactly the kind of place she had imagined for someone like Dr Merton.

Lydia, sensing Miranda's apprehension, offered a reassuring smile. "Don't worry, Miranda. Evelyn can be a bit intimidating at first, but she's fair and open-minded. Just be yourself."

Miranda nodded, grateful for Lydia's support. She knew that Lydia and Evelyn were close friends. When Lydia told Miranda she had recommended her for the dream job of Evelyn's research assistant, she had spent weeks preparing for this meeting, familiarising herself with Evelyn's work, and honing her arguments and ideas in anticipation of their conversation.

Evelyn greeted them at the door, her expression as composed as ever. She was a stately-looking woman in her early sixties, with sharp blue eyes that missed nothing. Her silver hair was pulled back in a tight, formal bun, and she wore a simple, elegant dress that reflected her no-nonsense attitude towards life. Miranda immediately felt under scrutiny from those piercing eyes as Evelyn took her measure.

"Lydia, it's good to see you…" Evelyn said warmly, giving Lydia a brief but affectionate hug. Then she turned her attention to Miranda. "… and Miranda, thank you so much for coming. Lydia does speak so very highly of you."

Miranda smiled, trying to project confidence despite the nervous energy bubbling up inside her. She suddenly became a more formal, much stiffer version of her normal self. "Thank you, Dr Merton. It's an honour to meet you. I've long admired your work, and I'm grateful for this opportunity to speak with you."

Evelyn inclined her head slightly, a gesture that Miranda took as an invitation to enter. Inside, the cottage was as charming and full of character as its exterior suggested. The scent of aged parchment and fresh herbs filled the air, creating a heady mix that only heightened Miranda's sense of awe.

The three women settled into the cosy sitting room, where a fire crackled softly in the hearth and the cats had arranged themselves around the room like furry scatter cushions. Lydia took the lead in initiating conversation, speaking of recent events in Exeter, updates on mutual acquaintances, and a few anecdotes that drew a rare smile from Evelyn. Miranda listened intently, observing the dynamic between the two older women.

As the conversation shifted towards more academic topics, Miranda found herself drawn into the discussion. When

Evelyn asked her about her recent thesis on the influence of Norman architecture on medieval Exeter, Miranda responded with passion and clarity. She spoke not just of the architectural styles and their origins but also of the social and cultural implications of these structures, tying them into the broader historical context. Evelyn listened closely, occasionally interjecting with a question or a counterpoint. Miranda handled these challenges with poise, demonstrating not only her knowledge but also her ability to think critically and adapt her arguments. Lydia watched with quiet satisfaction, pleased to see that Miranda was holding her own. What impressed Lydia most about Miranda was her ability to balance respect for Evelyn's experience with confidence in her ideas. Miranda did not simply echo what she thought Evelyn wanted to hear; instead, she engaged in a true dialogue, offering fresh perspectives while remaining open to Evelyn's insights. This was a delicate balance to strike, especially with someone as formidable as Evelyn, and Miranda managed it with grace.

As the afternoon wore on, the conversation grew more animated. The initial formality began to slowly melt away as Evelyn warmed to Miranda's presence. Miranda found herself increasingly at ease, her nerves giving way to genuine excitement. She was in her element, discussing ideas and theories with two women who shared her passion for history.

During their meeting, Miranda was particularly struck by how well Lydia and Evelyn worked together in conversation. There was an unspoken understanding between them, a kind of shorthand that came from years of friendship. Miranda admired this and hoped that she might one day develop similar relationships in her career. She was also acutely aware that she was being evaluated, not just by Evelyn but also by Lydia, and this realisation fuelled her determination to prove herself. She wanted an opportunity to work with Evelyn because it would be a significant step in her professional career.

Miranda's abilities were evident in everything she did that afternoon: she was attentive, engaged, and eager to contribute to the conversation. When Evelyn or Lydia spoke, she listened carefully, absorbing their words and responding thoughtfully. She made sure to reference specific works by Evelyn, demonstrating her familiarity with the material, and she wasn't afraid to ask questions or seek clarification when needed. She knew that part of being a good scholar was knowing when to listen and when to speak. In turn, Evelyn and Lydia loved the energy and enthusiasm that Miranda brought to subjects and conversations; it was very invigorating.

Miranda also demonstrated her commitment through her behaviour. One of the key moments of the meeting came when Evelyn, in a rare moment of candour, asked Miranda why she wanted to work with her specifically. It was a test, one that Miranda had anticipated but still felt a surge of anxiety when it came. She took a deep breath and answered with sincerity.

"Dr Merton, your work has been a source of inspiration for me since I first began studying medieval history. The way you connect historical events to broader social and cultural trends and how you bring to light the stories of those who might otherwise be forgotten. I would love to work with you because I believe I can learn a great deal from you, and because I want to contribute to the ongoing exploration of our shared history. I'm passionate about this field, and I'm eager to do the hard work necessary to make a meaningful contribution."

There was a long moment of silence after Miranda finished speaking, as if Evelyn were contemplating her reply. Then, slowly, she nodded.

"That is a good answer," Evelyn said, her voice measured. "Passion is important, but so is discipline. This work requires both. Are you prepared for that?"

Miranda met Evelyn's gaze and nodded. "Absolutely, Dr Merton. I understand, and I'm not afraid of hard work."

Evelyn studied her for a moment longer, then glanced at Lydia. There was something unspoken in the exchange between the two women, a brief communication that Miranda couldn't decipher. But whatever it was, it seemed to satisfy Evelyn.

"Very well," Evelyn said finally. "We'll see how you do. I will speak to HR about your contract..." she paused "...and please call me Evelyn."

As the meeting drew to a close, Miranda felt a mix of emotions of relief and elation. Evelyn walked Lydia and Miranda to the door. When Miranda stepped outside into the early evening, she felt a rush of exhilaration despite the rain that had got considerably harder. The meeting had gone well, better than she had dared to hope. More importantly, she had glimpsed a future that she desperately wanted to be a part of. The idea of working alongside Evelyn, of contributing to important historical research, filled her with a sense of purpose and direction.

As she walked back down the lane with Lydia, Miranda couldn't help but reflect on the events of the afternoon. She had been with two remarkable women, each of whom had left a significant impression on her. Lydia, with her warmth and subtle encouragement, had helped to put her at ease and had shown her the importance of building strong, supportive relationships in this field. Evelyn had challenged her in ways that made her realise just how much she still had to learn.

But more than anything, Miranda realised that this was just the beginning. She had proven to herself that she could hold her own in the company of brilliant minds, and she was more determined than ever to pursue her passion for history.

As they got in the car and out of the rain, Lydia, sensing Miranda's reflective mood, broke the silence. "You did well today, Miranda. I think Evelyn was impressed."

Miranda smiled, grateful for the affirmation. "Thank you, Lydia. I couldn't have done it without your support."

"Oh, nonsense," Lydia replied. "You're more capable than you allow yourself to believe, and you showed your true self today. Whatever happens next, just remember that."

Miranda nodded, feeling a surge of confidence. The meeting at Evelyn's cottage had been a test, and she had passed. Now, all that remained was to see where this new path would lead her.

Chapter 6

After a few days of rain, the late summer sun once again bathed Exeter's Cathedral Green in a glow that hinted that autumn was just around the corner, casting long shadows across the still-wet cobblestones. It was the kind of day that invited leisurely strolls and casual conversations. Lydia and Miranda walked side-by-side, their steps unhurried as they made their way toward Edward Voss's antiquarian bookshop.

Lydia had been surprised when Miranda told her she had never been to one of Exeter's most extraordinary establishments. Edward Voss's shop was known not just for its collection of rare books and manuscripts but also for the eccentricity of its owner. Lydia had lived in Exeter for many years and had visited the shop on many occasions, though she had never had more than a cursory exchange with Voss himself. She knew him to be a man of few words, a bit aloof, but she had no reason to expect anything unusual from this visit.

Miranda, on the other hand, was eager to explore the shop. As a young scholar, the prospect of finding a rare text or an obscure manuscript filled her with anticipation. She had heard of Edward Voss in passing and was aware that he had once worked with Dr Merton, but otherwise knew little about him. To her, he was simply another figure in the tapestry of Exeter's academic and cultural life.

As they approached the shop, Miranda noticed the

faded wooden sign hanging above the door, and her pulse quickened with anticipation. The display in the window was filled with an eclectic mix of books, aged and somehow inviting. There was a certain charm to the place, a sense of history that appealed to both women.

Lydia pushed open the heavy wooden door, and the bell tinkled above their heads. Miranda immediately noticed the smell of aged vellum and leather mixed with the dust picked out by the sunlight that streamed through the windows. It gave the feeling that the shop was a place frozen in time, in an era that matched the age of the books themselves rather than the hustle and bustle of the street outside.

Edward Voss was seated behind a large oak desk near the back of the shop, his attention focused on an ancient, leather-bound volume spread open before him. He didn't look up as the two women entered, but the slight stiffening of his shoulders suggested that he was aware of their presence. Lydia and Miranda exchanged a glance, both sensing the quiet intensity of the space.

Miranda was immediately struck by the sheer number of books surrounding her. The shelves were crammed with texts of all sizes, some neatly organised, others piled haphazardly, a cross between a jumble sale and an old library run by a lazy librarian. She felt a thrill of excitement – who knew what rare finds might be hidden among the stacks? Lydia, noticing Miranda's eagerness, smiled and gestured for her to explore while she approached the desk.

"Good afternoon, Mr Voss," Lydia said politely as she reached the desk. Edward finally looked up, his expression inscrutable as his eyes met hers.

"Ms Jones," he replied, his voice low and measured; he was well aware of her friendship with Evelyn. "What brings you to my shop today?"

Lydia was momentarily taken aback by the coldness in his tone, but she quickly recovered. "I wanted to show Miranda here your collection. She's a young scholar, working at the University on a project with Dr Merton related to medieval manuscripts. I thought she might find something of interest."

Edward's gaze shifted to Miranda, who was now browsing a nearby shelf. His eyes narrowed slightly as he observed her, and something flickered in his expression, something dark and unsettling. Lydia noticed the change and felt a prickle of unease; she couldn't quite place why, but there was something in the way Edward looked at Miranda that made her uncomfortable. Miranda, unaware of the scrutiny, was lost in her exploration of the shelves and cocooned in her favourite big coat. Her eyes scanned the spines of the books, admiring the craftsmanship and imagining the wealth of knowledge contained within. When she finally turned back toward the desk, she found Edward's gaze fixed on her. The intensity of his stare caught her off guard, and she hesitated and smiled nervously, unsure of how she should respond.

"Mr Voss," she began tentatively, "your collection is remarkable. I'm particularly interested in manuscripts from the medieval era about Exeter between the 13th and 1400s. Do you have any that might be available for study?"

Edward remained silent for a moment, his eyes never leaving hers. There was something in his stare that sent a chill through Miranda. His gaze was sharp, almost accusatory, as if he were evaluating her in some way.

"We have a few manuscripts that might interest you," Edward said finally, his voice devoid of warmth. "But they are rare and valuable. Not something I allow just anyone to handle."

Lydia, sensing the tension, stepped in. "Of course, Mr Voss. Miranda is a history graduate and an experienced researcher and would treat any text with the utmost care."

Edward's eyes flicked to Lydia, and for a brief moment, she thought she saw a flash of recognition, something that made her wonder if he knew more about the two of them than he let on. The moment passed, and his expression returned to its usual unreadable state.

"Very well," Edward sighed, rising from his chair. "I'll show you a few items, but you must be careful. These texts are, as I said, irreplaceable." He said the word irreplaceable syllable by syllable, as if for emphasis. Miranda nodded eagerly, though the chill in Edward's tone had dampened her natural enthusiasm. Lydia watched Edward as he led Miranda towards the back of the shop, noting the tension in his posture and the way he seemed to be holding something back, something that simmered just beneath the surface.

As Edward guided Miranda through the narrow aisles, showing her a few select manuscripts, his mind churned with conflicting emotions. On the surface, he forced himself to be calm and professional, but inside, his resentment was growing. He was taken aback by how meeting this student had stirred such a visceral reaction in him. Was it her youth? Was it because she worked with Evelyn? Or was it that she was becoming the academic he still longed to be?

At first, it had been Victoria, with her demanding presence and her powerful family, who had stirred these feelings of inadequacy and anger. Now, the connection between Lydia, Miranda and Dr Merton was triggering something far more sinister. The recognition had been almost immediate. Miranda's boundless enthusiasm and vivacity looking through his shop, which echoed Evelyn's passion, a glorious academic career ahead of her, further fuelled his bitterness. Then there was Lydia, seemingly so sure of herself. It galled him to think that she, with her calm authority, could be so closely associated with Evelyn.

The more Edward thought about it, the more his resentment grew. His anger wasn't just about Evelyn anymore; it was about everything he had lost, everything he had never achieved. The shop, the books, his knowledge of antiquities, these were his only sources of pride, but even they had been tainted by the failures of his past.

As Miranda continued to ask questions, Edward's answers became increasingly terse. Lydia, noticing the shift in his tone, felt her unease deepen. She had come to the shop expecting a pleasant visit, a chance to introduce Miranda to a respected antiquarian, but something was clearly amiss. Edward's mood had changed, and there was an undercurrent of hostility that she couldn't ignore. Miranda, too, began to sense that something was wrong. She had been so absorbed in the manuscripts that she hadn't initially noticed Edward's growing agitation, but now it was impossible to miss. His responses were clipped, his movements brusque, and his eyes held a hard edge that hadn't been there before.

The atmosphere in the shop had shifted from one of quiet intellectual curiosity to one of barely concealed tension. Lydia and Miranda exchanged uneasy glances as Edward's behaviour became more uncomfortable. Lydia decided it was time to bring the visit to an end. She had no idea what had triggered Edward's change in mood, but she sensed that it was best not to push any further. She glanced at her watch and then turned to Miranda.

"Miranda, we should probably be going. We don't want to take up too much of Mr Voss's time."

Miranda, though disappointed, nodded in agreement – she had no desire to linger. She carefully closed the manuscript she had been examining and placed it back on the shelf.

"Thank you for showing me these, Mr Voss," she said politely, though her voice was tinged with uncertainty.

Edward gave a curt nod, his eyes dark and unreadable.

"You're welcome," he said, though the words carried no sense; he would be prepared to help her again in the future.

Lydia and Miranda made their way back to the front of the shop, the silence between them weighed down with unspoken questions. As they reached the door, Lydia turned back to Edward, offering a polite smile.

"Thank you for your time, Mr Voss. We appreciate it."

Edward barely acknowledged her, his mind already elsewhere. The moment they left the shop, he would be alone with his thoughts once more, thoughts that grew bleaker by the minute.

As the door closed behind Lydia and Miranda, Edward stood in the centre of his shop, seething with anger. His small hands clenched into fists at his sides as he struggled to contain the torrent of emotions raging within him. The visit had dredged up memories and feelings he had long tried to bury, and now, to have these two women in his shop, felt like a cruel twist of fate.

Edward's resentment had grown over the years, simmering just beneath the surface, but today's visit had brought it all to a boiling point. He felt trapped, suffocated by the ghosts of his past. The shop, which had once been his sanctuary, was now filled with reminders of everything he had lost and not achieved.

With a growl of frustration, Edward swept a pile of books and irreplaceable manuscripts off the desk, sending them crashing to the floor. The sound echoed through the shop, breaking the oppressive silence, but did little to calm his anger. He wanted to lash out, to destroy something – anything – to relieve the pressure building inside him. He picked up one of the manuscripts he had been showing Miranda and tore it to shreds. Moments later, he realised what he had done in his rage and fell to his knees, trying to pick up the tiny pieces of vellum and place them back on the desk like putting together an ancient jigsaw puzzle, tears silently trickling down his cheeks.

There was nothing he could do; he was powerless, trapped in a life spiralling out of his control. Evelyn was gone, Victoria remained a constant source of resentment, and now, even these two women, whom he barely knew, had become symbols of his failures and resentments.

As Lydia and Miranda walked away from the shop, neither of them spoke for a long while. The visit had left them both feeling uneasy, though neither could fully articulate why. Miranda was disappointed: what should have been an exciting exploration of rare books had turned into an uncomfortable encounter with a man who seemed to display such a deep-seated anger.

Lydia, on the other hand, couldn't shake the feeling that something was seriously wrong with Edward Voss. She had known him to be eccentric, even aloof, but today he had been different: he seemed volatile, unpredictable.

Finally, Miranda broke the silence. "That was…strange," she said, her voice hesitant. "Mr Voss seemed…angry. Do you think we did something wrong?"

Lydia shook her head. "No, Miranda. I don't think it was anything we did. I think…Mr Voss is dealing with something very personal. Something of a trauma that has nothing to do with us."

Miranda frowned, still troubled by the encounter. "I hope he's okay. He seemed so…unhappy."

Lydia placed a comforting hand on Miranda's shoulder. "Don't worry about it. Whatever it is, it's not our responsibility. We'll just have to be careful if we need to visit the shop again."

Miranda nodded, though the uneasy feeling lingered. She couldn't shake the sense that there was more to Edward Voss than met the eye, something dangerous lurking beneath the surface.

Chapter 7

Detective Inspector Whipton Barton was a man of routine, and nothing brought him more peace than his daily walks with his Golden Retriever, Pip. On their early walk, they would walk down through the town of Topsham, the soft grey hues of dawn picking out the details of the buildings; then down to the Quay where they would stop and watch the river for a few minutes. The tide was very high and mirror flat today. The River Exe changed with the seasons, not only the colours and temperature, but also the number of boats moored there. Right now, the river was full of yachts and yawls as the summer sailing season was not yet complete.

After the Quay, they would walk back along the river path, past The Passage House Inn, which was so quiet in the mornings compared with the buzz of chatter that came from the people sitting at the tables on summer's evenings. This was a time and place of peace and reflection for him, a stark contrast to the often gritty realities of his work as a detective. The morning mist hung low over the water and the reeds, the town now waking up slowly, the main street still empty, apart from the occasional dog walker and the odd shopkeeper opening up early. Barton and Pip were always the first to take in the day, enjoying the tranquillity before the town got busy.

At this time of day, Pip didn't need to be on a lead, and he trotted beside his master, his golden coat gleaming in the soft light, his nose ever so slightly wet as he sniffed at the fresh scents of the morning, and his tail gently wagging as they walked. Pip was a dog of remarkable character, and everyone in the town recognised him. Barton often thought that more people knew Pip's name than they did his own. A friendly, loyal dog, brimming with an energy that was only fully expended on these walks. He lived for these moments of freedom, where the vastness of the open sky and the expanse of the river were his to explore. But more than that, Pip lived for Barton. The bond between man and dog was undeniable, forged through years of companionable walks and countless cases solved together. Though Pip couldn't speak, his presence was a constant source of comfort and unwavering support for Barton, especially in trying times.

This particular morning, Barton was free as his previous case had been sent to the CPS and Detective Sergeant Saxon Brooks, one of his junior officers and a tech wizard, was sorting through the final paperwork. Pip, ever attuned to his master's moods, sensed the lack of tension in Barton's steps, as if he were anticipating a longer walk than usual. The detective's stride was steady, and Pip nudged Barton's hand with his nose, a gentle reminder that he was not alone, and a treat would be a very good thing right now. Barton smiled faintly and reached down to give Pip an affectionate pat on the head. "Good boy, Pip," he murmured. "Shall we go the long way home?" As if he understood, Pip's tail wagged more vigorously as they headed into the Rec and Barton slipped him a treat from his pocket.

At that moment, Barton's phone rang; when he saw it was Brooks, Barton muttered, "This better not be about paperwork..." Then he stopped in his tracks as Brooks interrupted his thoughts. Pip, sensing the shift in Barton's mood, picked up a stick from the ground and playfully dropped it at his feet, with an extravagant play-bow, his tail wagging expectantly, looking up at Barton as he distractedly picked up the stick and threw it far into the distance. Pip happily blundered after it with the enthusiasm of a puppy, his ears flopping as he ran while Barton continued to listen to the scant details of the next case on the call. He ended the conversation with a promise that he would meet Brooks at the Chapter House in about half an hour and an instruction to make sure the crime scene was not disturbed by the forensics team before he arrived.

For a brief moment, Barton allowed himself to enjoy the simple joy of watching his dog at play, a welcome distraction from the grim report he had heard on the call. Pip never returned with the stick. In the distance, he looked at Barton with an air of, "Why would you throw away such a beautiful stick?" The detective couldn't help but think that with his dog, the retriever was in name only. Pip often accompanied him on investigations, his presence bringing a sense of ease to both Barton and some of those he interviewed. There was something about a dog's innocent, non-judgmental eyes that made people open up, sharing details they might otherwise keep to themselves. Perhaps, Barton mused, Pip could sometimes be able to sense something he could not, some detail that had been overlooked.

"Sorry, Pip, change of plan – straight home, then off to work." Their walk continued, but the pace quickened, the silence between them companionable, broken only by the occasional shout from a gull or the distant hum of the motorway. Barton's mind wandered to Brooks, his trusted colleague and friend. Brooks was a solid officer, detail-driven and determined, but he had never been one to warm to animals. Pip, however, had taken a particular liking to Brooks, much to the sergeant's bemusement. Despite Brooks's initial reluctance, he had come to accept Pip's affections, if not always returning them with the same enthusiasm. Pip, undeterred, seemed to have made it his mission to win over the stoic sergeant, often greeting him with a wagging tail and a hopeful look when their paths crossed.

Barton allowed a smile to himself, thinking of the unlikely friendship between his dog and Brooks. In many ways, Pip was like an ambassador of goodwill, breaking down barriers and bringing a bit of lightness to the often bleak work of solving crimes. Barton knew that having Pip around was as much for his benefit as it was for the dog. His responsibilities as a detective could be overwhelming at times, but Pip's unwavering loyalty and infectious enthusiasm were constant reminders that there was more to life.

"We'll solve this, Pip, but this is a weird one," he said quietly, more to himself than to the dog. "We always do."

Pip looked up at him, his brown eyes full of devotion. He didn't understand the complexities of the world his master navigated, but he knew that as long as they were together, everything would be all right. And in that simple, unshakeable belief, Barton found the strength to keep going, to face the challenges ahead.

Barton knew he could not take Pip to a crime scene; the amount of dog hair he shed every day would contaminate a crime scene on their arrival, and they could be interviewing every blonde in town for days.

Barton heard his wife starting her day and called up to let her know Pip was back in the kitchen and he had to be off as a body had been found at the Chapter House.

Chapter 8

It had been a cool early morning when the body was discovered. Daylight was just starting to break through the clouds, casting a soft grey light over the ancient stones of Exeter Cathedral. The city was trying to wake up, and the streets were still quiet, with only the distant sounds of birds chirping and the occasional car passing by. Inside the Cathedral, the atmosphere was one of tranquillity, as it had been for centuries.

Thomas Jones, a retired clergyman, now the Cathedral's long-serving custodian, discovered the body. He had always been an early riser, and it was his job to open up the Cathedral each morning and do his regular inspection rounds, ensuring that everything was in order before the first visitors arrived for Matins. He took his duties very seriously; he had always loved the Cathedral and followed a strict daily routine. On this morning, as he made his way through the quiet cloisters, he noticed something unusual: the door to the Chapter House, which was usually locked at night, didn't need unlocking. Had he missed this on the previous night's lock-up? That was highly unlikely, but he supposed not impossible, although he had never missed anything like this before. He stopped and listened to see if there were any sounds of movement. The more he listened, the quieter the Cathedral seemed to be.

Frowning, Jones approached the door, his keys jingling in his hand. He pushed the door open and stepped inside, expecting to find nothing more than a stray piece of paper or a misplaced book. Instead, he found something far more unsettling.

There was the woman he had seen so many times in the Chapter House, stock still on a chair by a desk with books and manuscripts all over it, feet solidly on the cold stone floor, about halfway down the length of the room. At first sight, she could have just been asleep, until you noticed the body was slightly twisted at an unnatural angle. Her face was pale, almost waxen, and her eyes stared blankly at the ceiling, the stillness of the body matching that of the statues in the alcoves arranged around the walls. Thomas shuddered. He had no idea of her name; she was dressed in what Jones would later describe as 'Devon countrywoman daywear'– a sensible skirt, stout walking shoes and a tailored blazer over a white high-collared blouse with a floral patterned silk scarf held in place by a broach at her neck. In some ways, the scene seemed oddly peaceful.

For a moment, Jones stood frozen in the doorway, his mind struggling to process what he was seeing. Then his instincts took over, and he rushed forward, dropping to his knees beside her. He reached out to touch her arm, but it was cold to the touch, too cold. With trembling hands, he checked for a pulse, but there was none.

Jones stumbled to his feet, his heart pounding in his chest. He ran out of the Chapter House to a place in the Cathedral where he knew he could get a signal. As he ran, he fumbled for his phone and dialled the emergency services, his voice shaking as he told the operator what he had found. Had he looked back, he would have seen a figure slip out of the Chapter House and into the shadows of the cloisters, head to the south transept. Within fifteen minutes, the Cathedral was swarming with police, the peace shattered by running footsteps and voices, the crackle of radios and orders being given. Incident tape was set up at the Chapter House door, and until the scene was released, anyone entering would have to be wearing scene-of-crime suits.

The Chapter House, a long oblong room located on the south side of the Cathedral, was a place of reflection and study. It was where the Cathedral's canons would gather to discuss matters of importance, and where scholars would often spend hours poring over ancient manuscripts and records. On this particular morning, however, the peaceful atmosphere of the Chapter House was shattered by the discovery that would set the entire city on edge once the news got out.

As the first officers on the scene began to secure the area, one question loomed large in everyone's mind: how had she been able to get into the Chapter House after lock-up? The door was always locked at night, and only a handful of people had access to the key, including Thomas Jones himself.

Jones was quick to tell the police that the door had been locked the previous evening, as it was every night when he did his rounds. The Cathedral was always closed to the public after the evening service, and he had made sure that all the doors were securely locked before he left for the night. There had been no sign of forced entry, and the key was still on his keyring, where it had been all night.

The only other people who had access to the Chapter House were the Dean of the Cathedral and a few other high-ranking members of the clergy. They were all very quickly accounted for and claimed to have been nowhere near the Chapter House the night before; all were mystified as to how the body had got there. It was a mystery that would only deepen as the investigation progressed.

DI Barton and DS Brooks arrived at the Cathedral shortly after the initial call. Barton, the seasoned detective, with a sharp mind and a calm personality, and Brooks, his tech-savvy younger colleague, made a formidable team.

As they entered the Chapter House, they were struck

by the contrast between the serene beauty of the room and the grim reality of what had happened there. The morning light filtered through the huge stained-glass window, casting colourful patterns on the stone floor. The sculptures in the alcoves around the walls gave the room an air of stillness, only now matched by the body in the centre of the room propped up at one of the desks as Jones had described, a stark reminder of the tragedy that had taken place.

The crime scene was carefully cordoned off, with forensic officers awaiting the Inspector's arrival as he had requested. In a few minutes, they would be photographing the scene and collecting evidence. Barton and Brooks always liked to look over the scene before anything had been moved. They took the initial details from a uniformed officer who had been first on the scene; by chance, he had been walking through the Cathedral Green at the end of his shift when the call came in. Then the two detectives looked into the Chapter House from behind the incident tape, their trained eyes noting the position of the body and the overall state of the room.

"There's no obvious sign of a struggle," Barton observed, his voice low as he spoke to Brooks. "Everything seems to be in its place, except for those books. They look like they have been arranged rather than how they would be if someone were using them for research."

Their next move was to put on their shoe coverings and overalls and venture into the room itself. Brooks crouched down to get a closer look at the books. "These look more like manuscripts she could have been studying. I wonder who she is?"

"She does seem familiar," Barton replied. He looked around the room, his mind racing with possibilities. "It looks like she collapsed suddenly."

"But why and how was she here in the first place?" Brooks asked, standing up and glancing at the only door. "If the door was locked, how did she get in?"

"That's what we need to find out," Barton said, his expression thoughtful. "But first we need to find out who she is."

There was no bag or phone next to the body, and her pockets appeared to be empty.

The duty pathologist, Jim McIntire, always referred to as Dr Jim, arrived shortly after Barton and Brooks, and they watched as he began his preliminary examination of the body. The skin was pale, with no visible signs of injury. There were no obvious indications of foul play, no bruises, no cuts, nothing to suggest that she had been attacked. But there was something odd about the way her body was positioned.

"She's been propped up. I would normally expect a body to be slumped forward," the pathologist noted, his voice clinical as he spoke. "Her arms are by her sides, and her legs are straight. I would expect them to be bent. I would say she was placed here."

"She looks familiar, Jim, but I can't for the life of me place her. There doesn't appear to be anything to identify her here," said Barton

"I can't be sure," said Jim, "but she looks like Dr Evelyn Merton from the University."

"Oh my God, of course. She is – was a good friend of my wife. It never fails to amaze me how a dead body somehow loses the identity of the living." Jim nodded.

Barton frowned and paused for a moment. "What do you mean, ' she was placed,' Jim?"

The pathologist gestured to the body. "It's not a natural position for someone who's collapsed. Usually, if someone falls, their body is in a more disorganised position, arms flailing, legs bent. But she's lying here almost as if she were arranged this way, a bit like a mannequin."

"That's strange," Brooks said, his brow furrowing. "Could she have been moved after she died?"

"It's possible, but would have to have been soon after

death," the pathologist replied. "But we won't know for sure until we do a full autopsy. What I can tell you right now is that there's no obvious cause of death. We'll need to run some tests to find out more."

"Keep us updated," Barton said, nodding to the pathologist. He turned to Brooks, his expression serious. "We need to find out everything we can about what Dr Merton was working on, or if she was meeting someone, and why she was here last night. There's more to this than meets the eye."

At that moment, Brooks, who had been staring intently at the body, spotted something. It was a tiny corner of what looked like a piece of coloured paper sticking out of the breast pocket of the jacket. He pointed out Barton and Dr Jim. Jim took out his tweezers and carefully extracted the piece of paper. It was a Post-it note that had been folded many times. On it was typed, "The past is a shadow that shapes the present."

"Why would she keep this with her?" asked Barton.

"Perhaps she didn't," replied Brooks, "Perhaps it was put there."

This last thought hung in the silence of the room, only broken by the murmuring of the forensic team and the clicking of the shutters of their cameras as they started to photograph every detail of the Chapter House, the body and the books.

A little later, Edward Voss arrived at his usual time, regular as clockwork, to open his shop; he didn't seem surprised to see the police. If anyone had been close by, they may even have seen the faintest, briefest smile cross his face as he started to unlock the shop door.

Chapter 9

According to the Cathedral staff, Dr Merton had been seen late the previous afternoon working in the archives, as was usual for her on a Thursday. She had spoken briefly with a few of them, but nothing seemed out of the ordinary. She usually had left the Cathedral around 6 pm if she had followed her usual routine and then gone home for the evening. No one had seen her again until her body was discovered by Thomas that morning. One thing was sure: they would need to interview her assistant as she was almost certainly one of the last people outside the Cathedral to see Dr Merton alive.

The crime scene forensics squad were still working hard in the Chapter House, so Barton and Brooks left and headed for the University. As they drove through the city and up onto the University Campus, the atmosphere changed from that of a city to that of a seat of learning. They found their way to the history department and, after showing their warrant cards to several folk, were admitted to the room where Dr Merton had worked.

Just outside in the open plan part of the office sat her assistant, Miranda Jackson, with her head down, obviously deep in thought. Brooks was taken aback by how young she seemed; she was dressed in a long, boldly coloured and patterned dress over a T-shirt, and she was wearing Dr Martens boots, her leather satchel hanging off the back of her chair. She had a real sense of style about her. Eventually, she became aware of the two men standing by her desk, and she looked up and took off her headphones.

"Excuse me, Ms Jackson, please, could we have a word in private?" They introduced themselves and showed their warrant cards, which she examined thoroughly.

"It's probably best that we speak in Dr Merton's office," she said, grabbing her satchel and leading them in. Once she had closed the door, she pointed them to two seats and then sat in what must have been Dr Merton's chair while the two officers sat on the much harder chairs usually occupied by visitors or students. Miranda sat back across the desk from Barton, her hands elegantly placed on the arms of the chair. Startled by the intrusion into her day, her large green eyes darted around the room, avoiding Barton's gaze. She had been Evelyn Merton's research assistant for nearly three months, a position of which she was proud.

"How can I help you?" she said in a rather clipped tone.

"Has Dr Merton been in the office today?" asked Barton

"No, I am not expecting her until this afternoon." Miranda looked suspiciously at him.

"Have you heard from her this morning?"

"No, I wouldn't expect to."

"I am sorry to have to say this, Ms Jackson," said Barton, "but this morning we found a body in the Chapter House at the Cathedral, and we believe it may be that of Dr Merton." The colour instantly drained from Miranda's face; she ran her hands through her hair, and tears started to fill her eyes.

She briefly pulled herself together to say, "That is awful... awful."

Barton could see from her face that this was news of the worst kind, and he said, "Ms Jackson, it would really help if you could come to the station with us so we can ask you some questions. Your boss seems to have been a very private person, and we could do with finding out more about her.

We don't yet know the cause of death, but we hope to have more information later today." She nodded, and as they left the office, she absent-mindedly started gathering her things from her desk and putting them in her satchel.

"Am I a suspect?" she asked, her mind racing, struggling to process all possible permutations of the situation she was now dealing with.

"No, Ms Jackson – you will be just helping us," said Brooks.

They drove back to Exeter police station in silence and a little later found themselves in a small, stark interview room. The fluorescent lights hummed faintly, casting a harsh glow over the metal table that separated DI Barton from Miranda Jackson. A tape recorder sat between them, its red light blinking steadily, so it could capture every word, every sigh, every nervous pause. The soundproof walls of the room seemed to close in, deadening any echo and making their voices sound as though they were slightly muffled, amplifying the silence that stretched between each question and answer.

DI Barton leaned forward slightly, his expression unreadable. He had only been leading the investigation for a few hours, and as yet, they didn't have a single solid fact with which to work. Miranda had obviously been devastated by the news of her boss's death, and Barton was aware that she was potentially looking at losing her job as well. His questions were deliberate, methodical, designed to extract information as gently and with as much detail as possible.

"Thank you for coming in to speak with us, Ms Jackson," Barton began, his voice steady and calm, though there was an underlying intensity to his words. "I know this must be an extremely difficult time for you, but we must understand everything that happened in the days leading up to Dr Merton's death."

Miranda nodded quickly, her voice shaky as she replied, "Of course, Inspector. I'll do whatever I can to help."

"Good," Barton said, flipping open a notebook and clicking his pen. "Let's start with how long you've been working for Dr Merton and what you can tell me about your time with her?"

Miranda took a deep breath as she tried to recall the details of her employment with Evelyn. "I started working for Dr Merton around three months ago," she began. "It was right after I finished my master's degree. I was looking for work, something related to my studies. I had become friends with another researcher, Lydia Jones, who is – was friends with Dr Merton, and she told me that Dr Merton was looking for a new research assistant. It was my dream opportunity. Dr Merton was so well respected in her field. I never imagined I'd be able to work alongside someone like her."

Barton nodded, jotting down notes as Miranda spoke. "And how did you find Dr Merton as a boss?"

Miranda hesitated, her gaze dropping to her hands as she twisted them in her lap. "She was…brilliant," she said slowly. "Intelligent, driven and passionate about her work. She could be demanding at times, but that's because she has – had – such high standards. She expected a lot from herself and from those who worked with her. I have learned so much from her in just three months, more than I could have ever learned in any classroom."

Barton watched her closely, noting the careful choice of words. "Demanding, you say. In what way?"

Miranda swallowed hard, feeling the pressure of the question. "Well, she wasn't the easiest person to work for," she admitted. "She could be very particular about how things were done. Everything had to be perfect in every detail, every citation, every translation. If something wasn't up to her standards, she wouldn't hesitate to let you know. Sometimes she could be…critical, but I knew it wasn't personal. It's just the way she is…" she paused again. "…Was."

"Did that ever cause any tension between the two of you?"

Barton pressed, his tone still even but probing.

Miranda shook her head quickly. "Not really. I mean, there were times when I felt frustrated with myself, but that's normal in any new job, right? Overall, I respected her and the work we were doing. It was challenging, but that's what made it rewarding."

Barton nodded, making another note. "When was the last time you saw Dr Merton?"

Miranda's brow furrowed as she thought back to the last time she had seen her boss alive. "It was yesterday, late afternoon," she said quietly. "We were working here, going over some documents for a project she was leading. She seemed normal, focused on the work. I didn't notice anything unusual."

"What was the project you were working on?" Barton asked, his eyes narrowing slightly as he considered the possibilities.

"It was a personal project that she kept entirely to herself. She was handing me notes and telling me where to file them. I don't know any more than that, other than I saw the name *Vita Regis*," Miranda explained. "Dr Merton had been researching the subject for years, and she was getting ready to publish a major paper on it. We were reviewing some original manuscripts she had acquired, trying to verify their authenticity and interpret some of the more obscure passages."

Barton made another note, then looked up at Miranda.

"On a completely different note, please could you let me have the address of the cottage? It seems not to be in the paperwork that has arrived from the University." Miranda nodded. "I guess there is no need for Dr Merton's need for secrecy anymore. For some reason, she was very protective of her address, but she never told me why." She jotted the address on a piece of paper." She sighed.

"And how had Dr Merton been acting in recent weeks? Anything out of the ordinary?" Barton continued.

Miranda bit her lip, thinking carefully. "She had seemed a little more stressed than usual," she admitted. "The project was so important to her, and she was under a lot of pressure to ensure everything was correct before she published. Other than that, she seemed fine. Maybe a little more distant than usual, but I just assumed it was because of the workload."

"Distant in what way?" Barton asked.

Miranda hesitated again. "It's hard to explain," she said slowly. "She wasn't as talkative as usual. She kept to herself more, didn't share as much about what she was thinking or planning. But I didn't think much of it at the time. I figured she was just focused on the project."

Barton considered her words, wondering if there was more to Dr Merton's behaviour than Miranda realised. "Did she mention anything that might have been worrying her? Any conflicts, concerns, or anything that might have been on her mind?"

Miranda shook her head. "No, nothing like that. She was always very private about her personal life. We mostly talked about work. If something was bothering her, she didn't share it with me. We had become more friendly recently, and we had been meeting at her cottage on a Sunday afternoon to plan the week, so we also chatted about other things too, but she was usually asking about my life rather than the other way round. She was really nice when you got to know her."

Barton leaned back in his chair, tapping his pen thoughtfully against his notebook. "And where were you last night?"

Miranda's green eyes widened slightly, and she shifted uncomfortably in her seat. "I was at home," she replied quickly. "I live in a small flat near St David's station. I had been working with Dr Merton all day, and after I left the office, I walked straight home. I didn't leave the flat again that night. I was so tired I even ordered a takeaway to be delivered."

"Can anyone corroborate that?" Barton asked, his tone neutral but the question pointed.

Miranda's cheeks flushed slightly, and she shook her head. "I live alone. But I am sure the takeaway company could confirm that I wasn't anywhere near the Cathedral that night, I swear."

Barton nodded, making another note. "What time did you leave the office?"

"It would have been between 5.30 and 6 pm," Miranda replied. "We had finished going over the documents, and she told me I could go. I offered to stay and help with anything else she needed, but she said she was done for the day and that she'd see me this afternoon."

Barton tapped his pen against the notebook again, thinking. "Did you notice anyone else around when you left? Anyone unusual hanging around the University?"

Miranda frowned, trying to recall. "No, I didn't see anyone. The campus is always pretty quiet when the students are away, and it was quiet when I left. I didn't think anything of it."

Barton made a final note, then closed his notebook and looked directly at Miranda. "Ms Jackson, is there anything else you can tell me about Dr Merton? Anything that might help us understand what happened to her?"

Miranda shook her head, tears welling up. "I wish I knew, Inspector," she said, her voice almost a whisper. "She was an incredible woman, and I can't believe she's gone. I don't understand why anyone would want to hurt her."

Barton studied her for a moment, weighing her words and her emotions. Miranda seemed genuinely distraught, but he knew that grief could sometimes mask other emotions, guilt, fear, even complicity. He would need to verify her whereabouts, and there were still many questions left unanswered. But for now, he had gathered as much as he could from her.

"Thank you, Ms Jackson," Barton said, his voice softening

slightly. "I appreciate your cooperation. We'll be in touch if we need any more information, and if anything occurs to you, please call me."

Miranda nodded, standing up shakily as Barton stood to see her out. She looked exhausted, the news of the day clearly taking its toll on her. Barton walked her to the door, watching as she left the interview room and was escorted down the corridor by a uniformed PC.

As he returned to the interview room and gathered his notes, Barton couldn't shake the feeling that there was more to Dr Merton's story than Ms Jackson was letting on or even knew. She had seemed sincere, but there were gaps in her account, gaps that needed to be filled if he was going to get to the bottom of Dr Evelyn Merton's death.

Back in his office, Barton spread out his notes on the desk, reviewing everything Miranda had told him. There were a few key points that stood out, details that might seem innocuous on their own but could hold more significance when viewed in the context of the investigation.

First, there was Miranda's description of Dr Merton as demanding and critical. While it was clear that Miranda had respected her boss, was there an undercurrent of tension in her words? Could that tension have escalated into something more serious? Barton made a note to dig deeper into her working relationship with Miranda. He had spoken to a few of the other members of Dr Merton's department during the day. But on the surface, she seemed well-liked, but very few were friends with her outside of work.

Then there was the project that, according to Miranda, had stressed Dr Merton and distant in recent weeks, *Vita Regis*, whatever that was. Apparently, Dr Merton had been working on it for years, and Barton wondered if the pressure of the project had been too much for her, or if there was something else, something unrelated to the work, that had been weighing on her mind.

Miranda had also mentioned that Dr Merton had acquired some original manuscripts for the project. Barton wondered if those documents could have played a role in her death.

And then there was the matter of verifying Miranda's movements. She had claimed to be home alone on the night of Dr Merton's death, but without any witnesses to corroborate her story. He would need to get her phone records checked by Brooks, and he could also hunt for any CCTV footage near her flat. Luckily, there were a few CCTV cameras around the University and St David's area.

Finally, there was the question of why Dr Merton had been at the Cathedral the night she died. Barton knew that the Chapter House was not open to the public after hours, which meant that Dr Merton had either been there with someone's permission or had gained access through other means.

As Barton pieced together these fragments of information, a picture began to form in his mind: an incomplete picture, but one that suggested there was much more to this case than a simple death. The more he learned, the more he was convinced that Dr Merton's death had not been an accident, suicide or the result of natural causes. There were too many unanswered questions, too many loose ends that didn't quite fit. He hoped the post-mortem report would reveal the first clear clues.

And then, there was the unsettling feeling that had nagged at him throughout his interview with Miranda – was there something she was holding back? Whether it was out of confusion, respecting Dr Merton's desire for privacy or something else entirely, Barton couldn't say, but he knew he needed to find out.

This was just Day One of the investigation; there were many more people to speak with, many more leads to follow. As he prepared his next move on the investigation, Barton couldn't shake the feeling that the answers he sought were closer than they appeared, hidden just beneath the surface of the seemingly ordinary lives of those connected to Dr Merton.

This evening, he would have to have a conversation with Lydia to see if she could shed any light on Dr Merton. As it was not generally known yet, it would also mean he would have to break the news of the loss of her friend.

He went to Saxon's office to get him to start checking Miranda's movements on the evening of the murder. Saxon Brooks was a tech wizard, a self-confessed nerd, and this sort of investigation of media, CCTV and missed connections was when he was at his happiest. He was so much better at this than he was with people.

Chapter 10

Barton had been dreading this moment since Dr Jim had identified the body as that of Dr Evelyn Merton. Barton had dealt with countless cases, each with its own set of challenges and tragedies, but this one hit too close to home. The death of Evelyn Merton was not just another case; she had been a close friend of Lydia's; he knew the news would devastate her, and he braced himself for the difficult conversation ahead.

It was late in the evening when Barton finally made his way home. The sky outside had turned a deep indigo, and Topsham was quiet, the usual business of the day giving way to the stillness of the night with just a couple of pubs and bars remaining busy. As he walked up the path to their cottage, Barton felt a sense of foreboding. He had spent the day combing through evidence and trying to piece together what had happened to Evelyn. But now he had to set aside the investigator and become the husband, the bearer of heart-wrenching news.

Lydia was in the kitchen when he entered the house. Pip came bounding into the hall carrying his favourite toy, wagging his tail so vigorously that his whole rear end seemed to be joining in the wag. The comforting aroma of home-cooked food wafted from the kitchen, a stark contrast to the cold reality Barton had been immersed in all day. Lydia was stirring a pot on the stove, her greying auburn hair loosely tied back, a few stray strands framing her face. She looked up as Barton entered, her face brightening at the sight of him.

"You're home late," Lydia said with a warm smile, but her expression quickly shifted to concern as she noticed the weariness in Barton's eyes. "Is everything alright, Whip?"

Barton took a deep breath, knowing there was no easy way to do this. He crossed the kitchen and gently took Lydia's hand in his, leading her to the small table by the window. He could feel the tension in her grip as they sat down, the unspoken worry already taking hold.

"Lydia," he began softly, his voice heavy with sympathy, "there's something I need to tell you. It's about Evelyn."

Lydia's eyes widened, her grip tightening on his hand. "Evelyn? What about her? Has something happened?"

Barton nodded, his heart breaking as he saw the fear and concern in Lydia's eyes. "I'm so sorry, Lydia. Evelyn was found today...at the Cathedral. She...she's gone."

For a moment, Lydia simply stared at him, her mind struggling to process the words. "Gone?" she repeated, her voice barely above a whisper. "You mean...she's dead?"

Barton nodded again, his own emotions threatening to overwhelm him too. "Yes. We don't know all the details yet, but it appears that she died last night. We're still investigating, trying to piece together what happened."

Lydia's face crumpled, and a sob escaped her lips as the reality of Barton's words sank in. She covered her mouth with her hand, tears welling up in her eyes. "No...no, not Evelyn," she whispered. "She can't be gone. She was...she was so full of life."

Barton reached out and took Lydia into his arms, holding her close as she wept. He could feel her body shaking with grief, and all he could do was hold her, offering what little comfort he could in the face of such a profound loss.

"I'm so sorry, Lyd," Barton murmured, his voice choked with emotion. "I know how much she meant to you."

Lydia clung to him, her tears soaking into his shirt as she struggled to comprehend the sudden loss of her friend. "She was like a sister to me," Lydia whispered, her voice breaking. "We shared so much...our hopes, our dreams, our secrets. I can't believe she's gone, Whip. I can't believe it."

Barton closed his eyes, feeling the weight of Lydia's grief as if it were his own. He knew there was a strong bond between Lydia and Evelyn that had grown from their collaborations in research, although he had never actually met Evelyn in person. The way they had supported each other through life's challenges, celebrated each other's successes, and shared the deep, unspoken understanding that only true friends possess. Losing Evelyn was like losing a part of herself, and Barton knew that the pain Lydia was feeling would not easily fade and never really go away.

They sat there in silence for a while, Lydia's sobs gradually subsiding as Barton held her, his presence a steady anchor in her storm of emotions. Eventually, Lydia pulled back slightly, wiping her tear-streaked face with the back of her hand.

"How...how did it happen?" Lydia asked, her voice hoarse from crying.

"We're still trying to work that out," Barton replied gently. "There were no obvious signs of foul play, but it's too early to say for certain. We're waiting for the results of the post-mortem. She was found in the Chapter House at the Cathedral, and we're trying to figure out how she ended up there."

Lydia nodded slowly, her mind racing as she tried to make sense of it all. "The Cathedral?" she murmured, more to herself than to Barton.

"We don't have anything to go on yet," Barton said, his tone cautious. "But I promise you, Lyd, we'll find out what happened to Evelyn."

Lydia looked up at him, her eyes still glistening with tears, but there was a determination in her gaze that hadn't been there before. "Evelyn was always so careful, so precise," she said softly. "She did go to the Cathedral often on a Thursday, but wouldn't have gone there without a reason, but what was that reason?"

Barton nodded, knowing that Lydia's insight could be invaluable to the investigation. "That's why I need your help, Lyd," he said gently. "You knew Evelyn, probably better than anyone. If there's anything, anything at all, that you can think of that might help us understand what happened, it could make all the difference."

Lydia took a deep breath, trying to push through her grief to focus on the task at hand. "Evelyn was very private, even with me," she began. "She had a way of keeping things close to her chest, especially when it came to her work. But there was something different about her lately, something that seemed to be bothering her."

Barton leaned forward slightly, his interest piqued. "What do you mean?"

Lydia hesitated, trying to find the right words. "Evelyn was always dedicated to her research, but recently, it was like she had become obsessed. She spent more and more time at her cottage, poring over documents, manuscripts, anything she could get her hands on. She wouldn't talk about what she was working on, not in the way she usually did. She was... secretive. And it wasn't like her."

"Secretive how?" Barton pressed, his mind already turning over the possibilities.

Lydia shook her head, frustration flickering across her face. "I don't know. She would say things like, 'It's better if you don't know,' or 'I'll tell you when the time is right.' At first, I thought she was just being dramatic, but now with this...Now I wonder if she was trying to protect me from something."

Barton's brow furrowed as he considered Lydia's words. Evelyn's fixation on privacy, the secrecy surrounding her recent work, could it all be connected to her death?

"Did she mention anything specific? Was there something in her research that could have put her in danger?" Barton asked, his tone gentle but probing. "Any names, places or documents that seemed to be particularly important to her?"

Lydia frowned, trying to recall the conversations she had had with Evelyn in the weeks leading up to her death. "She mentioned something about a manuscript she was trying to authenticate," Lydia said slowly. "I didn't get the details, but she seemed really excited about it. She said it could change everything we thought we knew about a particular period in medieval history. But she wouldn't say more than that."

Barton made a mental note to look into any recent acquisitions Evelyn might have made. If this manuscript were as important as Evelyn believed, it could be a crucial piece of the puzzle.

"Anything else?" Barton asked, his tone encouraging.

Lydia bit her lip, her expression troubled. "There was one more thing," she said quietly. "About a month ago, Evelyn confided in me that she felt like she was being watched. She didn't say much, just that she had this sense that someone was following her, keeping tabs on her. I told her she was probably just stressed, but now...Now I wonder if she was right. I wonder if someone had got wind of her mysterious research project. I just wish I knew more about it"

Barton's heart skipped a beat at Lydia's revelation. The possibility that Evelyn had been under surveillance added another layer of complexity to the case. Who would have been watching her, and why? Was it connected to her research, or was there something more sinister at play?

"Did she say anything about who might have been watching her?" Barton asked, his tone careful.

Lydia shook her head, her frustration evident. "No, she didn't. She just brushed it off, said it was probably nothing. But it wasn't like Evelyn to be paranoid. She was always so grounded, so logical. If she felt like something was wrong, then maybe it was."

Barton nodded, understanding Lydia's concern. If she had felt that she was being watched, there was a good chance that she was right.

"I'll make sure we look into that," Barton said, his voice firm. "If there was someone following Evelyn, we'll find out who it was and why."

Lydia looked at him, her eyes filled with a mixture of hope and fear. "Do you really think you'll be able to find out what happened to her, Whipton?"

Barton reached out and took Lydia's hand, giving it a reassuring squeeze. "I do," he said with conviction.

Lydia nodded, taking comfort in Barton's words. But even as she did, she couldn't shake the feeling that Evelyn's death was like a puzzle with too many missing pieces.

As the evening wore on, Barton and Lydia continued to talk, and Pip's warm body was arranged across their feet as he slept contentedly, snoring sonorously. Piecing together Lydia's memories of Evelyn, they tried to make sense of the tragedy. They spoke of Evelyn's brilliance, her passion for history and her unwavering dedication to her work. They also spoke of her quirks, her fixation on privacy and the mysterious project that had consumed her in recent months.

Barton listened intently as Lydia shared her insights, his mind working overtime to connect the dots. He knew that the answers they sought were out there, hidden in the shadows of Evelyn's life.

Barton asked Lydia about Miranda, and she was effusive about her energy, knowledge and delight at the opportunity of working with her academic hero. She also talked about their friendship, some of the walks they took around Exeter, and how they had met. For Lydia to speak so warmly about a colleague and friend made Barton think again about Miranda's interview. Had she held anything back, or was she just stunned into shock by the news and not able to articulate her thoughts in such a stressful situation? He would need to talk to her again.

Lydia, worn out by the emotion of the evening, decided to have a relaxing bath and go to bed. Barton's mind, however, was racing, processing the conversation of the evening and trying to put it into context with the day's work. He knew sleep was an impossibility, so he stood up, and Pip looked hopeful. "Come on then," said Barton, looking down at his faithful dog, already curled up in his bed. There was a slight questioning wag, but he didn't move until Barton picked up his lead. This was the best thing that had happened to Pip since the last walk, apart from, of course, food, company and a walk with Lydia. For Pip, life was good and supremely uncomplicated; perhaps that was why he was always so happy.

They left the cottage quietly and walked down the narrow street towards the river. At this time of night, there was no one around, even the swans were asleep on the slipway. The only sound was Barton's footsteps and Pip's paw pads on the tarmac of the Underway. They sat down at the benches and watched the dark water lap against the edge of the path, the church wall behind them still warm from being in the sun most of the day. Barton thought about Lydia's comments about obsessive privacy and standards at work and how they mirrored Miranda Jackson's answers to his questions.

Then he moved on to the soon-to-be published work that he knew Dr Merton had been working on, that her closest friends and colleagues know so little about. The phrase "better you don't know" also kept buzzing around his head. After a while in quiet contemplation, they got up and continued their walk, Pip shambling along beside him as they walked past the riverside pub, now dark and silent after the evening session. They turned up the hill and back into the high street, where it was so quiet it felt like the town had been evacuated. When they reached the house, they let themselves in quietly.

Pip headed to his basket and curled up and was asleep in one smooth action; Barton had intended to do the same, but sleep took a little more time to arrive.

As he lay in the dark, with Lydia sleeping fitfully beside him, his mind raced with possibilities. He knew that the days ahead would be difficult. He had rarely worked on a case with so much information but with so few strong leads. The investigation was already fraught with challenges and obstacles. He also knew that he would be questioned about the progress of the investigation both at work and at home. As he closed his eyes and finally drifted off to sleep, one thought remained: the truth was still quite a long way from being uncovered.

Chapter 11

The next day, Barton got a call from the Exeter Mortuary: the preliminary post-mortem was complete, and could he come in to discuss it with Dr Jim? Interesting, thought Barton, usually the preliminaries were just emailed to him – did this mean that the doctor had found something significant?

Post-mortem examinations were conducted in the sterile, brightly lit room. For Barton, it was crucial to understand how the renowned historian had met her untimely end. He stood at the edge of the room, his arms crossed as he watched Jim draw back the sheet covering the body.

"Evelyn Merton was found in the Chapter House of Exeter Cathedral," said the doctor for the benefit of the recording," an unusual place for someone to be alone at night. The circumstances of her death are mysterious. The preliminary findings at the scene have offered little in the way of answers," Jim continued.

He now began to note points of significance, his voice steady and clinical. "There are no obvious signs of trauma, no lacerations, no contusions that would suggest a violent struggle," he said. "However, I'm noticing some slight unusual discolouration on her fingertips and around her lips."

Barton stepped closer, frowning as he looked at the lips. "What do you make of it?" he asked.

Jim paused, considering the possibilities. "It could be a sign of poisoning, but it's difficult to say without further tests.

The discolouration is subtle, almost as if whatever caused it was meant to be concealed."

Barton's interest was piqued. Poisoning was a plausible cause of death, but it raised even more questions. Who would have wanted to poison Evelyn, and why? And how had it been administered?

Jim now began to talk about the examination of her organs. "When we inspected Evelyn's organs," his brow furrowed in concentration, "there was something strange," he murmured, more to himself than to Barton.

"What?" Barton asked, his voice edged with urgency.

Jim looked up, his expression serious. "Her lungs. They show signs of acute pulmonary oedema, fluid accumulation that suggests she may have experienced severe respiratory distress before she died. But what's unusual is the lack of any clear cause. There are no signs of infection, no obvious obstruction."

Barton's mind raced as he considered the implications. "Could it have been an allergic reaction?" he suggested.

Jim shook his head. "Possibly, but there's something else. Her heart is slightly enlarged, and there's evidence of arrhythmia, which could indicate she suffered a cardiac event. But again, there's no clear cause. It's almost as if her body just...failed," he sighed.

"I found traces of a substance on her tongue. It's faint, but it appears to be some kind of powder, possibly a drug."

Barton's eyes narrowed as he processed this information. "Could that have been what caused her death?" he asked.

"It's possible," Dr Jim replied. "But we'll need to analyse the substance to know for sure. If it is a drug, it could explain the cardiac symptoms and the respiratory distress. I am running a full toxicology screen, but I suspect it might be something that's not easily detectable. If this was poisoning, it wasn't done with a common substance. Whoever did this knew what to use to conceal what they had done."

Barton felt a chill run down his spine. Evelyn Merton's death was becoming more and more enigmatic with each passing moment. "You don't think she took whatever it was herself? Said Barton.

"Highly unlikely, as there was nothing left at the crime scene that contained a poison, nothing in her water bottle." A silence fell between the two men as they thought through the implications.

Barton's thoughts were interrupted by Jim's voice. "If it is poison, then this is certainly murder." The words seemed to echo around the room. "There's one more thing," he said, his tone grave, "This would also mean that Evelyn Merton had been deliberately targeted, her death carried out by someone with a plan."

As he left the mortuary, he had a call from Saxon.

"Miranda Jackson's story checked out; several neighbours had seen her entering her flat that evening, and her phone records showed she hadn't left during the night. Additionally, CCTV footage from her building's entrance corroborated her story, and they had also seen the delivery driver and could clearly see him hand the takeaway to Miranda. She had indeed been at home.

Barton sighed with relief. Miranda had seemed sincere during their interview, and now he had confirmation that she had been telling the truth. However, this now left him with another more difficult question: who wanted Dr Merton dead?

Barton wanted to talk to Miranda again now to find out more about Dr Merton; he gave her a call, and she agreed to come back to the police station.

Miranda arrived at the station early the following morning, looking slightly more composed than the last time Barton had seen her. She was still ashen, her eyes showing signs of fatigue; he suspected she hadn't slept much, but this morning she seemed more determined.

"Thank you for coming in again, Miranda," Barton said as

he gestured for her to sit.

"I know this is a very difficult time for you, but I have a few more questions that I hope you can help me with."

Miranda nodded, her hands relaxed in her lap. "Of course, Inspector. I want to help in any way I can."

Barton leaned forward slightly, his expression serious but not unkind. "OK, when we first spoke, you mentioned that Dr Merton had been acting differently in the weeks leading up to her death. Can you tell me more about that? Anything specific you remember?"

Miranda took a deep breath, her gaze distant as she recalled the details. "Dr Merton was always very focused on her work, but recently, she had become distracted – like it was an obsession. She was working late into the night, often not leaving her office until the early hours of the morning. She barely slept, barely ate. I was worried about her, but every time I tried to talk to her about it, she changed the subject."

Barton listened intently, his mind piecing together the puzzle. "When we first spoke, you mentioned the *Vita Regis*. Is the anymore you can tell me about this?"

Miranda hesitated. "She was so secretive about it, even with me. I know it had something to do with a manuscript fragment she had recently acquired. She said it was a significant find, she wouldn't say more than that."

It seemed to Barton that this manuscript could be a key that may unlock the case, but why had Evelyn been so secretive about it?

"Did she mention where the manuscript had come from?" Barton asked, his tone probing.

Miranda slowly shook her head. "No, she only said that it had come from a private collection and that she was sworn to secrecy about its origins. She was adamant that no one could know about it until she had verified its authenticity."

Barton frowned, sensing that there was more to this story. "Miranda, is there anything else you can think of? Anything at all Dr Merton said or did that seemed out of the ordinary?" People who may resent her success? People she may have offended in the course of her work. People in her personal life, past or present, who worried her?

Miranda looked down at her hands, her expression troubled. "No, not really, she was generally liked. There is one thing, though," she said quietly. "About a week before she died, Dr Merton mentioned that she felt like she was being watched. She said it in passing, almost as if she was joking, but I could tell it was bothering her. I asked her if she wanted me to stay with her, but she insisted she was fine. Now, I can't help but wonder if there was more to it."

Barton's mind raced as he considered Miranda's words; this matched what Lydia had said last night. The feeling of being watched, the secretive work on the manuscript, the strange symptoms found in the post-mortem, everything was starting to point to a calculated plan, one that had been carefully crafted to eliminate Evelyn without leaving any obvious clues. Who would go to such lengths to silence her? And what was it about that manuscript that had put her in danger?

As the interview came to a close, Barton could see that Miranda was still deeply affected by Evelyn's death. But there was something else about her now, as if she had resolved to find out the truth, no matter what it took.

"Inspector," Miranda said as she stood to leave, her voice steady but tinged with emotion, "I've been thinking a lot since our last conversation. There's something that keeps nagging at me, something I can't shake. I don't know if it's important, but I feel like I have to tell you."

Barton looked at her, his interest piqued. "What is it, Miranda?"

"It's about the last time I saw Dr Merton alive," she said slowly. "There was something in her eyes, something I've never seen before. I think it was fear, but also...regret. Like she knew something terrible was going to happen, and she couldn't stop it."

Barton felt a shiver run down his spine. "Regret about what?" he asked.

Miranda shook her head, her expression pained. "I just don't know, but I think it may have had something to do with that manuscript. Whatever it was, it was something she couldn't resolve. I just wish I knew what it was."

"I have one last question I would like you to think about. Does this quote mean anything to you: 'The past is a shadow that shapes the present.' Was this important to Dr Merton?

"It doesn't ring any bells, but I will go through my notes and see if it has been said and I have forgotten. She then looked Barton in the eye and said, "It may be worth talking to Lydia about it. I am sorry, I had no idea Lydia was your wife when we last spoke; I only just put two and two together last night. She knew Dr Merton much longer and much better than me."

Barton watched as Miranda left the room, his mind swirling with yet more questions. Evelyn Merton's death was more than just a tragic accident or a random act of violence. It was part of a much larger puzzle, one that was becoming increasingly complex with each new piece of information.

As Barton prepared to delve deeper into the case, he knew that the answers they sought were somewhere out there. Barton and Brooks went through the interview notes and post-mortem and then decided that the next person to officially interview was Lydia. With Dr Merton having no immediate or contactable family, Lydia was the only person who could possibly fill in some of her background.

Chapter 12

The official interview with Lydia was conducted in the quiet, dimly lit study of their home. The room, filled with shelves of books and papers, exuded a sense of comfort and familiarity. However, the mood was anything but light. Lydia sat across from her husband and his colleague, DS Brooks, who was recording the interview and making notes. She took a deep breath as she prepared to discuss the life of her late friend. Pip had settled at her feet, and the warmth of his body against her legs was somehow reassuring. It was strange, yet oddly comforting, doing something this official in her home.

Lydia's connection to Evelyn had made this case more than just another investigation for Barton; it was deeply personal. He knew that Lydia's insights could provide critical information about Evelyn's life, her work and perhaps even the reason behind her untimely death. He started the conversation gently, understanding the emotional toll this discussion would have on Lydia.

"Lydia," he began, his voice soft but steady, "I know this is difficult, but anything you can tell me about Evelyn could help us understand what might have led to her death. Let's start with her past. How did you two meet?"

Lydia took a deep breath, her eyes filled with sorrow. "We met about ten years ago at an academic conference on medieval history in Exeter. Evelyn was presenting a paper based on her book *Invisible Women: Gender and Power in Medieval England*, a topic I was particularly interested in as a researcher myself. I was immediately struck by her passion and depth of knowledge. I went up to her after her presentation, and from that moment on, we became at first colleagues and then friends."

She paused, recalling the early days of their friendship. "Evelyn had this energy about her, a kind of intellectual vibrancy that drew people to her. She was also private, guarded in a way. She didn't let many people get close to her, but once you were in her circle, she was fiercely loyal."

Whipton nodded, taking notes as he listened. "What about her past? Did she ever talk about her family or her childhood?"

Lydia's brow furrowed as she considered the question. "She only mentioned her family very occasionally. From what she told me, she grew up in a small village near Oxford; her parents were both academics: her father was a historian, and her mother was a literature professor. She was an only child, and they were both supportive and very demanding. I think that's part of why she was so driven in her own career."

"She never spoke much about her childhood beyond that," Lydia continued. "It was clear that she had a complicated relationship with her parents. She once told me that she felt like she was always living in their shadows, trying to prove herself. I think that's why she became so dedicated to her work. It was her way of carving out her own identity, separate from them. I am pretty sure neither is still alive."

Whipton noted the significance of this. A strained relationship with her parents might have been a source of unresolved tension in Evelyn's life. "What about other people? How did colleagues and acquaintances react to her?"

Lydia sighed, her expression pensive. "Evelyn was respected, even admired, in academic circles, but she was also feared by some of the junior researchers. She had a reputation for being incredibly exacting and demanding. She didn't tolerate mediocrity, and she had little patience for those who didn't share her level of commitment. Some people found her intimidating, but those who worked closely with her knew that she was fair – if you met her high standards, she would go out of her way to support you."

"But", Lydia added, "there was also a loneliness about her. She was so consumed by her work that she didn't have much of a social life. I think that's why our friendship was so important to her. We would spend hours talking about history, of course, but also about life, about our hopes and fears. She confided in me, I think, in a way that she didn't with others."

Whipton had never fully realised the sisterly bond Lydia and Evelyn had shared. "Did she ever mention any concerns or worries in those conversations? Anything that might have been troubling her recently?"

Lydia hesitated, her eyes flickering with uncertainty. "There were a few things, yes. Evelyn was always concerned that her work could be stolen or misused. I often wondered if that was the reason she never had romantic relationships was that she didn't want anyone getting too close to her or her work. However, in the last few months, this seemed to grow into paranoia. At first, I thought she was just being her usual cautious self, but as time went on, it became clear that she was genuinely afraid."

"She also mentioned receiving some unsettling messages," Lydia continued, her voice tinged with concern. "They were anonymous, and she never told me exactly what they said, but they shook her. I urged her to go to the police, but she refused. She said she didn't want to draw attention to herself or her work."

Whipton felt a surge of frustration. If only Evelyn had come forward with those messages, perhaps things could have turned out differently. "Did she ever share what she was working on during those last few weeks? Something that might have been worth killing for. Do you know if she kept any of the messages?"

Lydia bit her lip, thinking carefully. "Evelyn was incredibly secretive about her latest project. All she told me was that the manuscript she had recently acquired had changed everything, something that could potentially rewrite a significant part of medieval history. She was thrilled about it and, at the same time, very guarded. She didn't even want to discuss it in detail with me, which was unusual. Normally, she would have been eager to share her excitement. I am afraid I don't know anything more about the messages. If she did keep them, I suspect they would be in the cottage. I don't think she would have risked them being found at work."

The mention of the manuscript piqued Barton's interest. This had been a recurring theme in the investigation so far. "Did she tell you where she got the manuscript?"

"No," Lydia replied, shaking her head. "She was very tight-lipped about it. She only said that it had come from a private collection and that she was under strict instructions not to disclose its origins to anyone until she had verified its authenticity; it was important that its existence was kept between them. She seemed almost…" she hesitated, searching for the best description, "protective of it, like it was her responsibility to keep it safe, as if she was its custodian."

Barton jotted down more notes, feeling the pieces of the puzzle starting to come together. Evelyn's paranoia, the mysterious manuscript and the unsettling messages, there was a picture emerging, one that seemed may point to a serious threat to Evelyn's life being connected to the current research.

"Let's talk about Miranda Jackson," Barton said, shifting the focus of the conversation. "Evelyn's assistant. How did you meet her, and what was your impression of her?"

Lydia's expression softened slightly as she recalled her first meeting with Miranda. "Miranda and I had first met when we were waiting for the same document at the archive about a year ago. Evelyn had recently mentioned how much she missed having an assistant, but she had lost confidence in her judgment in employing one after the previous assistant left. Although that was over ten years ago, I got the impression it ended badly. Evelyn hired Miranda as her assistant after they first met when I took her to see Evelyn at the cottage. I think this may have been because I had recommended and introduced her. She seemed very pleased with her work. Miranda is young, very bright, and eager to learn. She has this contagious enthusiasm, and Evelyn seemed to enjoy mentoring her as well."

Lydia paused, her gaze distant. "But there was something else, too. Evelyn was protective of Miranda, almost as if she saw a bit of herself in her. I think she wanted to help Miranda in a way that she hadn't been helped when she was younger. She took Miranda under her wing, and in return, Miranda became her friend as well as her loyal assistant."

"Did Miranda ever mention any concerns or worries about Evelyn?" Whipton asked, curious about the dynamic between the two women.

"Not directly," Lydia replied, "but she did seem concerned about the pressure Evelyn was putting herself under. She mentioned once that Evelyn had been working late into the night, barely sleeping. Miranda tried to get her to take breaks, but Evelyn was too driven. She was obsessed with this manuscript and the research surrounding it."

Barton nodded, understanding the toll that such an obsession could take. "Did Evelyn ever express any doubts about Miranda? Any signs that she didn't fully trust her?"

Lydia shook her head. "No, if anything, she trusted Miranda more than anyone else. She relied on her for everything, research, organisation – sometimes she even ordered her food shop. I think Miranda became more than just an assistant to Evelyn…she became a confidante."

Barton absorbed this information, realising that Miranda's role in Evelyn's life was far more positive than it had initially appeared. "Did Evelyn ever talk about her plans for the future? What does she want to do once this research is complete?"

Lydia smiled sadly. "She had big dreams. She wanted to publish a groundbreaking book that would change the way we understand medieval history. She was already thinking about her next project, something related to women's roles in early religious movements. She was so full of ideas. It's hard to believe she's gone."

The room fell silent for a moment as both Barton and Lydia reflected on the loss of such a brilliant mind. But he knew that he couldn't dwell on the sadness.

"Lydia," he said gently, "is there anything else you can think of? Anything that might help us understand what happened to Evelyn?"

Lydia hesitated, searching her memory. "There is one thing," she said slowly. "A few weeks before she died, Evelyn mentioned something about feeling like she was being followed. She said it in passing, almost like it was a joke, but I could tell it was bothering her. I asked her if she was alright, and she just shrugged it off. But now, looking back, I think there may have been more to it."

Whipton's heart sank as he realised how close Evelyn had been to reaching out for help, only to keep her fears to herself. "Did she say who she thought was following her?"

"No," Lydia replied, her voice tinged with regret. "She didn't give any details. But I could see there was fear in her eyes. She was trying to stay strong, not to let it affect her work. It was clear that something, or someone, was making her feel threatened, but she wouldn't be pushed to give any more details."

Barton made a mental note to follow up on this lead. Whoever had been following Evelyn might be the key to solving her murder. "Thank you, Lydia," he said, reaching out to take her hand. "I know this hasn't been easy, but you've been a tremendous help."

Lydia squeezed his hand in return, her eyes filled with tears. "I just want to find out who did this, Whip. Evelyn didn't deserve to die – she was brilliant, and she had so much more to give. Please, find out who did this to her."

Barton nodded, I have one last question for now, Lydia. "Do you ever recall her using the quote 'The past is a shadow that shapes the present'?"

"I have never heard Evelyn mention it. I think it is from a South African book that offers a means to wrestle with and perhaps find peace with the ghosts of your own history. None of which would have been of any interest to Evelyn. Why do you ask?"

Barton said, "It was a message typed on a small piece of paper tucked into her jacket pocket."

"Could that have been put there by the killer rather than it belonging to Evelyn?" asked Lydia.

As they drove back to the station, Brooks had an idea. "Perhaps we should look into where she could have got or found this manuscript. I will start looking into other antiquarians across Devon first and widen it nationwide if I have had no success. We also need to search the cottage and Dr Merton's office again. I seem to be building quite a list of things we need to either find or disregard."

Barton nodded, his mind on the quote and Lydia's idea. Messages had turned up in other conversations. "Yep," he said. "You get on that, and we need to find evidence of these messages."

Chapter 13

The next day, Barton and Brooks stood on the front doorstep of Dr Evelyn Merton's cottage. The garden was a little overgrown, a tangled mass of wildflowers, herbs and shrubs and her two supercilious cats loitering in the undergrowth, oblivious to the interlopers. Barton hesitated for a moment before entering; he reflected that the hardest searches were the ones when you don't know what you are looking for. His investigation into Dr Merton's mysterious death had led him here, to this quiet, remote cottage, where he hoped to find something that would shed light on her, her final days and perhaps some sort of potential motive.

As he crossed the threshold, Barton was struck by the contrast between the exterior of the cottage and the warmth inside. The living room was cosy, filled with shelves that overflowed with volumes on medieval history, religion and literature. It was a very personal space, and Barton felt like an intruder, a voyeur even. The walls were lined with framed photographs and prints, many of them depicting historical sites, ancient manuscripts and artefacts from across Europe. It was clear that this was where Evelyn had spent countless hours immersed in her work, surrounded by the things she loved and souvenirs from her glittering career. It felt as if she had just popped out to buy a pint of milk and would be back any minute to resume her work.

Barton moved slowly through the room, taking in every

detail. He knew that the answers he sought might be hidden in the smallest, most inconspicuous places. He started with the bookshelves, looking along the spines of the books, many of which were cracked and tattered due to their age and the many readers over the years. Some were marked with small Post-it notes, sticky tabs peeking out from the pages where Evelyn had made annotations. Barton carefully pulled out a few of these volumes, flipping through the pages to see if any of her notes might be relevant to the case. The tiny handwriting, precise and neat, offered insights into her thought processes, but nothing that immediately jumped out as a clue.

Brooks had turned his attention to the desk that dominated one corner of the living room. It was an old, sturdy wooden piece, worn with age but still solid. The surface was cluttered with papers, notebooks, a USB drive and a few personal items, a framed photograph of Evelyn as a young woman standing in front of a Cathedral, a small jade statue, a cup full of pens and pencils. Brooks sifted through the papers, looking for anything that might hint at what Evelyn had been working on immediately before her death.

Among the papers, he found drafts of an article she had been writing, along with preparation notes for a lecture and some folders. But it was a small, leather-bound journal that caught Brooks's attention. The journal was well-worn, its thin pages filled with Evelyn's handwriting. As he flipped through the pages, he saw that it was a combination of a diary and a research log. On some pages, she had recorded her thoughts, observations and ideas, while others were more focused on her work, detailing her excitement over a recent discovery or her frustration with the academic establishment.

One entry in particular stood out. Dated just a few days before her death, Evelyn had written about the manuscript she had recently acquired, describing it as potentially groundbreaking. She mentioned her concerns about its authenticity and her plans to verify it. But there was something else: she wrote about feeling that someone was watching her, waiting for her to slip up. She didn't name anyone, but the fear in her words was palpable.

Brooks handed the journal to Barton as he was pretty sure it would be crucial to the investigation. He then continued to search the desk, opening each drawer and examining its contents. The top drawers held the usual office supplies, paper, envelopes, pens and the like. But the bottom drawer was securely locked.

Barton frowned and tried the handle himself to see if it would budge, but it remained firmly shut. He searched through the other drawers and the surface of the desk for a key but found nothing. It was clear that whatever was inside the locked drawer was something Evelyn had wanted to keep hidden or secret.

Barton made a note to return with the necessary tools to open the drawer. For now, he moved on to the rest of the cottage while Brooks was packing the folders and other papers to take with them.

The kitchen was small and functional, with a few pots and pans hanging from a rack and a kitchen table that was covered with more papers and books. It seemed that Evelyn's work had invaded every corner of her life, leaving little room for anything else. The single bedroom was similarly austere. The bed was neatly made, and the wardrobe held a modest collection of clothes, mostly practical, comfortable garments suited to long hours spent in libraries and archives. There was a very faint smell of a fragrance hanging in the air. A small dressing table with a mirror, where Evelyn had kept a few personal items, a bottle of perfume, a hairbrush, a small box containing a pair of earrings and a necklace. On the bedside table, Barton found another stack of books and a few more notebooks filled with Evelyn's notes.

It was the small, locked drawer in the desk downstairs that

continued to nag at Barton. Whatever was in there, it was something Evelyn had taken great care to keep safe. He also knew he was going to need Miranda's help to make head and tail of all the notebooks, folders and research, to, at the very least, put them into some sort of order; she may even know about where Dr Merton kept her keys. They locked up the cottage, loaded the evidence into the car and returned to the station.

The following day, Barton and Miranda met at Evelyn's University office. Miranda had been cooperative and willing to help, although Barton knew she was still deeply shaken by her mentor's death. As she went to put the key in the lock, Miranda hesitated, her hand trembling slightly.

"Are you alright, Miranda?" Barton asked.

She nodded, taking a deep breath. "It's just…so hard to believe she's gone. This office was like a second home to her. I haven't been able to bring myself to go back in since you told me she had died." Barton understood her hesitation.

Miranda unlocked the door, and they stepped inside. The office was small and ordered, much more so than the cottage, with shelves lined with books and folders, and a large desk that faced the window. Barton began by examining the desk, which was neatly organised with a computer, a few framed photographs and several stacks of papers. Barton noticed that the papers were arranged in a very particular colour-coded order, as if Evelyn had been in the middle of a number of projects. He carefully lifted each stack, skimming through the contents. Most of it was related to her ongoing research, drafts of articles, notes on medieval manuscripts, and correspondence with colleagues. There was nothing that immediately stood out as a clue. The bottom drawer was also locked, and with no obvious key in the office.

He moved on to the filing cabinet, tucked away in the corner of the room. Miranda at least had this key, and he opened the top drawer. The cabinet was filled with folders, each labelled and organised. Barton flipped through the drawer, noting the range of topics: medieval history, religious studies, and manuscript analysis.

As Barton worked his way through the drawers, he found a file that had been placed at the very back, almost as if Evelyn had been trying to hide it. The label read "Confidential: Personal." Barton opened the file and found a series of letters, all typewritten, presumably all from the same person. It looked like they had been written to her over several years, but never signed, so Lydia was correct, Evelyn had kept them, just not at the cottage.

The letters were troubling; the anonymous writer seemed obsessed with Evelyn. The tone of the letters grew increasingly erratic, shifting from admiration to anger, and eventually, to something threatening. The last letter accused Evelyn of "betraying" them, though it was unclear what the nature of this betrayal was.

"Did you know about this file?" Barton asked

She shook her head. "Dr Merton did most of her own filing and kept the filing cabinet locked. She always said that it was organised the way she liked it. The only reason I had a key was for emergencies." She paused, then, almost whispering to herself, "I suppose like now."

Barton thought through the implications: was this person who had been sending Evelyn the unsettling messages? Was this the same person she thought was following her, as Lydia had mentioned? Barton knew they had to find out the identity of the letter writer, but for now, he must continue his search.

He turned his attention back to the desk, focusing on the locked drawer. After yesterday, Barton had come prepared. Miranda watched anxiously as Barton produced a set of lock-picking tools. He had been shown how to do this by an old housebreaker when he was a young constable. He now worked quickly, and after a few moments, the lock clicked open. Inside the drawer, Barton found a few more folders and a USB drive.

Barton passed the USB to Miranda, and she plugged it into her computer, but all it displayed was a lock screen, requiring a password to access the files. Barton knew he would have to get Brooks on to this, and until he cracked the encryption, everything on the drive would remain a secret.

As Barton pieced together the information he had gathered from the cottage and the office, a picture began to form. The letters suggested some kind of relationship that had turned toxic. Maybe the encrypted USB drive could show something more, a secret that Evelyn had been trying to uncover, or perhaps, trying to protect.

Barton knew that he was only scratching the surface of a much deeper mystery. If Evelyn's death had not been a random act of violence, surely it must be connected to her work, her past and the people she had known. The key to solving the case lay in understanding the connections between all these elements, and unravelling the secrets that Evelyn had taken to her grave.

As they left the office, Barton knew the answers he sought were still just out of reach at the moment. It was like looking through a misty window: he was beginning to see some vague shapes on the other side, but as yet nothing was coming into focus.

Brooks was no stranger to encryption. He had spent years developing his skills in digital forensics, and he approached the task with the meticulousness of a surgeon. With the USB from the office, the moment he tried to open it, it was clear that it was unlike anything he had encountered before. The encryption was very sophisticated, excessively so, for academic work, raising his suspicions. The encryption had to have been crafted by someone with extensive knowledge of cybersecurity.

Unperturbed, Brooks pressed on, breaking through several more layers of encryption. Yet, each time he reached what he thought was the core of the data, he was met with more dead ends, nonsensical files, and random strings of numbers. Whoever had encrypted these files had gone to great lengths to ensure that nothing of value would be accessed. It was beginning to feel as if the files from the University were deliberately designed to waste his time.

As he dug deeper, he encountered still more sophisticated security measures, each layer more complex than the last. The encryption was not just a security measure; it was a game designed to frustrate and confuse. After hours of work, Brooks finally managed to open the drive. He was expecting to find notes, research papers. Instead, what he had found was a simple text file.

Brooks stared at the screen in disbelief. It was a taunt, plain and simple, something more fitting for a tech prank than the work of a serious academic. He had begun to suspect that these files had been encrypted not just to protect information but to distract and mislead anyone who tried to access them.

He called Barton, "I have managed to open the office USB. Barton was momentarily excited until Brooks said, "All it had was a file that said, 'Ha, ha, ha. You'll have to try harder than that.' I can't even tell who the document author was; it could have been Dr Merton, but this feels like we are being taunted by someone."

"Keep going, it may be that there are some genuine documents somewhere. See if you can open the one you found at the cottage next," said Barton.

A few seconds later, Barton's phone pinged with a text from Brooks, "Meant to say, complete blank on any manuscript fragment being sold to Dr Merton from anywhere across the UK through the usual channels. Perhaps this was more of a personal arrangement, so below the radar. Sorry. S"

Two other leads closed off, thought Barton.

Chapter 14

A couple of days later, Barton returned to Dr Merton's cottage, this time with Miranda, who was with him, ready to help sift through the mountain of paperwork he and Brooks had collected from the first visit to the cottage and from Dr Merton's office at the University.

Barton hoped that the cottage held the key to the investigation and that with Miranda's help they would be able to organise the material they had collected so far – and perhaps identify other useful papers from Dr Merton's home.

"Let's start with the desk drawer," Barton said, breaking the silence. "We couldn't get into it last time, but I've brought the necessary tools today." Miranda nodded, her eyes scanning the room as if searching for clues in the shadows. Barton could tell she was anxious. He approached the old wooden desk; the locked drawer had been a nagging presence in his mind ever since his last visit.

With a few deft movements, the lock clicked open, revealing its contents: a small stack of envelopes, another leather-bound notebook and a collection of photographs, neatly tied together with a ribbon. Barton carefully removed the items and set them on the desk.

He handed the photographs to Miranda, who took them hesitantly, as if afraid of what she might see. As she flipped through the images, Barton watched her closely, noting the slight furrow on her brow and the way her lips pressed together in concentration. She quickly realised that they were all of Evelyn with various groups of former students on projects. The photos seemed to span several years, showing these groups together at academic events and even a few personal gatherings. There were several photos of a young man who appeared important to Evelyn.

"These are…very personal," Miranda said softly. "I didn't know Dr Merton had these."

"Do you recognise anyone in the photos?" Barton asked, leaning closer to see for himself.

Miranda stared at the photographs for a long moment before nodding slowly. "Yes, I am pretty sure this one looks like it could be a young Edward Voss."

Edward Voss was a name that had started to recur in the investigation, one that now seemed to be gaining more significance. "Tell me more about him." Miranda set the photographs down carefully, as if they might shatter if she were clumsy.

"I've known the name since I arrived at the University, but had never actually met him until recently with Lydia. After that, I did a bit of digging, and it turns out that he also worked for Dr Merton, although he left about ten years ago. He was an academic, I believe, specialising in medieval history, and I gather they worked very closely for a while before he left quite suddenly."

The images showed Voss and Merton at various university events, smiling, sometimes leaning close as they discussed something of apparent mutual interest. There were also photos where there seemed to be an air of tension. "Whichever way you look at these, there *was* some apparent chemistry there," Miranda continued. "There were rumours that they were more than just colleagues, but Dr Merton was typically very secretive about her personal life."

Barton considered this information carefully. A former assistant, once close to Evelyn but later estranged, Voss seemed to be emerging as a person of interest in the investigation. The connection between them was too strong to ignore, and now, with these photos, there was a tangible link to their past.

"What can you tell me about Voss's time with Dr Merton?" Barton asked. "Any details, even the smallest ones, could be important."

Miranda paused, thinking back to her early days working with Dr Merton. "I don't know much about Voss's work directly, but I do know that Dr Merton was working on something significant during that time, a project she was very passionate about. After Voss left, she continued to work on the project herself."

"Do you have any idea what that project might have been?" Barton pressed.

Miranda shook her head. "No, she never shared any details with me. But whatever it was, it consumed a lot of her time and energy. This project seemed different, more personal, somehow."

Barton frowned, a secret project, a falling out with a former assistant, and now, a mysterious death. Maybe the pieces were beginning to fit together, but there were still too many gaps. "The notebook looks like a mix of personal reflections and work-related notes," Barton said. "It's hard to tell where one ends and the other begins. Rather like the one we found at the office."

Barton continued to read through the notebook, noting a few entries that stood out. There were references to a "betrayal" and a "loss of trust," though it wasn't clear who or what Evelyn was referring to. "This project," Barton said, looking up at Miranda. "It seems like it was very important to Dr Merton, almost like it was her life's work. Do you think Edward Voss could have been involved in it?"

"Well, I suppose it's possible," Miranda replied. "If they were as close as the photos seem to suggest, then it's likely that he was involved in some way in the early stages. Whatever happened between them must have been serious, because Dr Merton never spoke of any connections with Voss after he left."

Barton closed the notebook. "We need to dig deeper into Voss's past, find out more about his relationship with Dr Merton and what he's been up to since they parted ways; it could be the key to understanding what happened to her."

Miranda nodded, "Actually, while I was doing my own digging, I went to HR and asked for a list of Dr Merton's previous assistants. It wasn't easy to get, but I managed to persuade them that it was important for the investigation."

She pulled a folded piece of paper from her bag and handed it to Barton. "Here's the list, as you can see, it confirms Edward Voss was the assistant immediately before me, followed by a ten-year gap."

Barton unfolded the paper and scanned the names. Voss was listed as having worked with Dr Merton for about two years. The list also included brief notes about each assistant's role and their reason for leaving. Next to Voss's name, the note was terse and uninformative; it read: "Left to pursue independent research."

Barton frowned. "Independent research? That's rather vague, compared to the others."

"HR didn't have much more information than that," Miranda said. "But it struck me as odd, too. Most of Dr Merton's assistants either moved on to other academic positions or completed their studies. But Voss just…left."

Barton felt a growing sense of unease. "We need to find out what he's been doing since then. Is he still involved in academia, or has he completely left it behind? We also need to look into whether he had a connection to this mysterious project."

Miranda nodded. "You know Voss now runs the Antiquarian bookshop on Cathedral Green, and I think

I have seen him in the paper at some sort of society 'do.' I believe he is married to Victoria Berger."

Barton appreciated her dedication, but he also knew they had to be careful, in particular with any connection to the Berger family, who were hugely influential with friends in very high places. Whoever was behind Evelyn's death was likely to be someone with a lot to lose, someone who might be willing to go to great lengths to protect their secrets.

"Thank you, Miranda," Barton said. "Your help has been invaluable. But remember, we're dealing with someone who is obviously dangerous. If you notice anything unusual, or if you feel unsafe at any point, you need to let me know immediately." He passed her a card with his station number, but also his mobile number. "Anytime."

"I will," Miranda promised. "But I'm not going to back down. Dr Merton was more than just a mentor to me; she was my friend."

The rest of the day at the cottage was spent laboriously going through the remaining paperwork. Barton and Miranda worked in silence, occasionally exchanging thoughts or observations as they pieced together the fragments of Evelyn Merton's life. The papers that they sorted through included lecture notes, drafts of articles, correspondence with colleagues and more personal documents that only hinted at Evelyn's private life.

As they sifted through the papers, Barton found himself growing more intrigued by the woman who had lived in this cottage. Among the documents, they found more references to the mysterious project that had consumed so much of Evelyn's time and energy. There were notes on ancient manuscripts, sketches of medieval symbols and cryptic references to "the hidden truth." But nothing was concrete enough to provide a clear understanding of what Evelyn had been working on or why it might have led to her death.

Barton was particularly interested in a series of letters they discovered, written in Evelyn's distinctive handwriting but never sent. The letters were addressed to various colleagues and institutions, each one expressing concern about the integrity of her work and the possibility that someone was trying to undermine her research. The tone of the letters was anxious, as if Evelyn believed she was being duped.

"These letters...she was worried about something," Barton said, reading through one of the drafts. "But she never sent them. Why?"

"Maybe she didn't want to alarm anyone, or maybe she wasn't sure who she could trust," Miranda suggested. "If she felt isolated, she might have kept her fears to herself."

Barton nodded, considering this. "Or perhaps she was afraid that if she voiced her concerns, it would make her a target."

Miranda shuddered at the thought. "It's possible. But whatever she was worried about, it seems to have been connected to her work. These notes," she gestured to a pile of papers on the desk, "they all seem to point to something she felt was important enough to risk everything for."

Barton agreed. The more they uncovered, the more it seemed that Evelyn had been on the verge of a major discovery; there was also the possibility that this discovery had put her in danger, that someone had wanted to stop her before she could reveal whatever she had found. Was she undermining other academics' lifetime work?

After exhausting the paperwork at the cottage, they gathered together a mixture of journals, correspondence, photos, notes and other paperwork and drove back to the University.

Barton needed Miranda's help again at Dr Merton's office to help unravel her filing system. They went through the desk looking for connections to their findings from earlier that day, starting with the top drawers, which contained the usual office supplies and some personal items, nothing out of the ordinary. However, upon closer inspection of the bottom drawer, Barton found a locked compartment.

"This one looks more secure than the one at the cottage," Miranda observed as Barton examined the lock.

"Probably contains something important," Barton agreed. "Let's see what she was hiding."

After a few minutes, the compartment slid open. Inside, they found a small, black box with a digital combination lock. Barton raised an eyebrow, impressed. "Dr Merton really didn't want anyone getting into this." Miranda watched as Barton attempted to crack the code, a process that took several minutes of trial and error. Finally, the lock clicked open, and Barton carefully lifted the lid. 1066, he thought, not the most original combination, particularly for a history professor.

Inside, they found a neatly folded piece of paper. The paper contained a list of names, dates and locations. The names were all connected to prestigious academics and their institutions, and some of the dates went back several decades.

"This must be related to her research," Miranda said, looking over Barton's shoulder. "But why keep it locked away like this?"

"Because she knew it was dangerous?" Barton replied. "We'll need to check this list against the other documents and the USB drive from the cottage."

As they continued searching the office, they found more drafts of papers that Evelyn had been working on, including one that seemed to be an early version of an article she had published years ago. There were also inconsistencies, notes that suggested she had changed her conclusions as new data emerged, or perhaps under duress.

"Do you think someone forced her to change her work?" Miranda asked, her voice tinged with concern.

"It's possible," Barton said, considering the implications. "Or maybe she felt pressured by her ambitions. But either way, it looks like she was struggling with something, or someone, that affected her work."

Finally, they turned their attention to Evelyn's office computer. Miranda sat down at the desk, quickly navigating through the files. Barton was impressed by her skill; she clearly knew her way around a computer, and within minutes, she had accessed Evelyn's most recent documents.

"There's nothing unusual here," Miranda said, scrolling through the files. "Just the usual drafts and notes. But there is one folder that's password protected. Do you want me to try and open it?"

"Absolutely," Barton said, leaning in closer. "Let's see what she was trying to keep hidden."

Miranda typed quickly, attempting several passwords before finally gaining access to the folder. Inside, they found a further series of encrypted files.

"This one's labelled 'The Project'," Miranda said, opening one of the unencrypted files. "It looks like an index of her research."

Barton read over her shoulder, noting the references to ancient texts and symbols, as well as mentions of a hidden truth that Evelyn believed was buried deep in history. The language was vague, almost cryptic, but it was clear that Evelyn felt she had been onto something significant.

"We need to get into the USB drive from the cottage," Barton said, his mind racing with possibilities. "Whatever Dr Merton was working on, I think it's the key to understanding why she was killed. We know the drive from the office was a decoy, but the cottage one may be vital."

Miranda nodded, her face pale; she looked emotionally drained. Barton knew they were running out of time. Whoever was behind Evelyn's death would know that they were investigating, and he or she may strike again if they felt threatened, or perhaps they were treating this like a chess game, always keeping one or two moves ahead.

"I'll get back to the station and get Brooks started analysing the encrypted files and drives. We also need to keep a close eye on Edward Voss. I think he's more involved in this than we initially thought."

As they left the office, Barton couldn't shake the feeling that they were on the verge of a breakthrough. But he also knew that with every discovery, they were stepping deeper into the unknown. He needed Brooks to work his magic on the encrypted cottage USB drive. He needed to work out Voss's background and the connection with the Berger family. Given the family's position in the county, he was going to need to speak to his boss and get some advice or at least find someone he could talk to about the family without making them aware of the investigation.

Chapter 15

DI Barton made an appointment to see his senior officer on the way back to the station. As luck would have it, Chief Inspector Michael Dixon was available. He was the kind of man who straddled two worlds. He was equally at home at a black-tie event in the heart of Devon's county society as he was navigating the murky waters of a complex criminal investigation. His reputation had preceded him when he transferred to Exeter, and the general feeling among senior officers down to the lowliest constable was that the city was lucky to have him.

As Barton made his way to Dixon's office, nestled within the imposing walls of the Exeter Police Headquarters, he felt a sense of anticipation. The investigation into Dr Merton's death had taken several strange turns, and Barton hoped that Dixon might be able to provide a much-needed, objective perspective. The case had initially seemed to be a possible suicide, then shifted to murder as the evidence began to emerge; it now seemed to have deeper, darker secrets as to motive.

The office door was ajar when Barton arrived. Dixon's deep, resonant voice carried through the small gap as Barton could hear him finishing a phone call. He waited politely outside until Dixon's voice dropped and the call ended.

"Come in, Barton," Dixon called out, as if sensing his presence. "Door's open."

Barton pushed the door fully open and stepped inside. The office was spacious, one wall lined with bookshelves filled with criminology books, and various mementoes and awards from Dixon's long career. The large window behind Dixon's desk overlooked the city, the Cathedral just visible in the distance. On the other wall, a landscape painting of Dartmoor, a nod to Dixon's deep roots in Devon.

"Chief Inspector…" Barton greeted, nodding respectfully as he took a seat opposite Dixon's desk. "Thank you for seeing me."

Dixon waved away the formality with a smile. "No need to thank me, Barton. I've been following the Merton case closely. It's stirred up quite a bit of interest," He gestured to a coffee machine on the side table. "Care for a coffee? I find it helps clear the mind on days like these."

Barton hesitated for a moment, then nodded. "Why not? It's been one of those cases."

Dixon poured two cups of strong Italian coffee. "This will stimulate the senses," he said before settling back into his leather chair.

"Now," Dixon began, his eyes narrowing slightly as he focused on Barton, "tell me what's on your mind. I've read the early reports, of course, but I want to hear it from you. What's your gut feeling?"

Barton took a sip of his coffee, savouring its buzz as it spread through him. "My gut tells me we're dealing with something more than a straightforward murder," he said after a moment. "From the evidence so far, it seems that Dr Merton was working on something, something big. So far, we have found some encrypted files on her computer, a USB stick hidden in her office – that one was an elaborate hoax – and another USB we found at the cottage. I have a strong feeling that whatever she was researching might have been a motive for her death."

Dixon nodded, his expression thoughtful. "And this

Edward Voss character? What's your take on him?"

"By all accounts, he seems…something of a mysterious loner. Having said that, I haven't wanted to interview him until I have my thoughts straight. If it is him, he has thought this whole thing through in great detail and seems to be controlling the story so far," Barton replied, choosing his words carefully. "From what I've gathered, he's brilliant but troubled. He had a turbulent professional relationship with Dr Merton, and his departure from her employ was abrupt. There's also his marriage to Victoria Berger, and add to that Dr Merton's research into a fragmented manuscript that could rewrite history. It's a tangled web, Michael, and I'm not sure how all the threads connect, or even if I have all the threads yet, but I'm certain they do somehow."

Dixon leaned back in his chair, fingers tapping lightly on the armrest "You're right to trust your instincts, Barton. Cases like this often have layers, and those can hide all manner of sins. The academic world, especially at Merton's level, is a pressure cooker. Ambition, jealousy, intellectual property disputes, they can all lead to dangerous outcomes."

Barton nodded. "That's my thinking. But it's not just the academic rivalry. I suspect there's more at play. I suppose it may even involve the Berger family in some way. They're powerful, influential. If Voss was involved with Merton's death, it might have been to protect Victoria or something she was involved in. But I don't have any evidence linking them yet; that is all just a hunch."

Dixon took another sip of his coffee, contemplating Barton's words. "The Bergers are indeed a force to be reckoned with," he said slowly. "Leonard Berger has his fingers in many pies, and he's a man who values his family's reputation above all else. If Dr Merton had discovered something that could tarnish that reputation, it wouldn't be out of the realm of possibility that he would take drastic measures."

Barton's gaze sharpened. "You think Leonard Berger might

be involved?"

Dixon raised a hand, cautioning against jumping to conclusions. "I'm not saying that. But you must consider the possibility. The Berger family is a dynasty, and dynasties are built on secrets. Whether Leonard was directly involved or not, it's possible that his influence could have played a role."

There was a moment of silence as Dixon's words hung in the air. "But", Dixon continued, his tone more measured now, "before we dive too deeply into those waters, I suggest you focus on the facts. The project Merton was working on, what do we know about it? If we can understand why it was so important, we might be able to see the bigger picture."

Barton took a deep breath. "That's part of the problem. We just don't know exactly what she was working on. DS Brooks is working on the USB drive from the cottage now. We have had a lot of help from Miranda Jackson, Dr Merton's assistant, who knows as much as anyone about Dr Merton's work, and even she knows very little about the project."

Dixon's eyes narrowed. "That is quite vague. Do you have any specifics?"

"Not yet," Barton admitted. "But I've been piecing together bits and pieces. Dr Merton was obsessed with a particular period, late medieval to early Renaissance. She'd been corresponding with several experts in the field, including some overseas. There was mention of a manuscript fragment, something rare and possibly explosive–and maybe previously misinterpreted."

Dixon considered this, his brow furrowed in thought. "A manuscript, you say. That could be a lead. Ancient texts, especially those with religious or political significance, have been the cause of bloodshed before. If Merton had uncovered something that threatened to upset the status quo, I suppose that could be motive enough for murder."

Barton felt a flicker of excitement. This was exactly why he had come to Dixon: to gain insight from a mind that could be objective, to connect the dots in ways that can be missed by those in the middle of an investigation.

"Michael," Barton said, his voice tinged with urgency, "do you have any contacts in the academic world, someone who might be able to help us understand the significance of what Merton was working on?"

Dixon smiled a small, knowing smile. "As a matter of fact, I do. There's a professor at Oxford, Henry Lowman – I believe Dr Merton was one of his students at Balliol way back. He's one of the leading experts in the field. If anyone may have the ability to shed light on what Dr Merton might have been involved in, it's him. I'll arrange an introduction."

Barton felt that this could be the break he needed to understand the background to Dr Merton's research. "Thank you, Michael. I'll set up a call or meeting with him."

"It will probably be a face-to-face meeting. Lowman doesn't have much time for online communications; you will end up driving to Oxford to see him. Unless he has undergone a major character change very recently."

Dixon nodded but then leaned forward, his expression growing serious. "One more thing, Barton. Be careful. If Voss is involved, and if the Bergers have a stake in this, you're treading on dangerous ground. People in their position don't take kindly to threats, real or perceived. And if they feel cornered, they may react in ways you don't expect."

Barton met Dixon's gaze, understanding the gravity of the situation. "I know. But I have to follow the evidence, wherever it leads."

"That's what makes you a good detective," Dixon said. "But don't go it alone. I'll help where I can, and I'll put you in touch with Lowman. If you need someone to watch your back, don't hesitate to ask. There's no shame in leaning on your colleagues."

Barton felt a deep sense of gratitude for Dixon's support. The older man had years of experience, and his advice was invaluable. "I appreciate that, Michael. I really do."

Dixon finished his coffee and put the cup down on his desk with a decisive click. "Good. Now, let's clarify how we're going to proceed. First, I'll reach out to Lowman and brief him on the situation. Then, you should pay a visit to Voss, see if you can rattle his cage a bit, and get a sense of what he knows. And we'll need to keep a close eye on Victoria Berger."

Barton nodded in agreement. "I'll also dig deeper into Dr Merton's personal life. There might be someone who knows more about her state of mind in the weeks leading up to her death. We have already established she had no immediate family, so it could be my wife and Miranda are the only sources for now."

"Good thinking," Dixon said. "And Barton, remember to trust your instincts. They've served you well so far, and they'll continue to do so."

Barton understood Dixon's warning; the case was becoming increasingly personal, especially with Lydia being one of Dr Merton's closest friends. He knew that emotions could easily cloud even the best detective's judgment. Dixon smiled, a warm, reassuring smile that put Barton at ease. "Good man. Now, let's get to work. We've got a mystery to solve, and I have a feeling that the answers are closer than they appear right now."

The two men rose, and Dixon walked Barton to the door. As Barton stepped out into the corridor, he felt a renewed sense of purpose. As he made his way out of the building and into the bustling streets of Exeter, Barton's mind was buzzing with all the possibilities.

Chapter 16

The darkness of the early morning hours in Pinhoe was usually still and peaceful, interrupted only by the occasional hoot of an owl or the distant rumble of a passing train. On this particular night, the serenity was shattered by the sudden, violent blaze that erupted from Dr Evelyn Merton's cottage. The flames licked the sky with such ferocity that they turned the quiet night into a chaotic scene of flickering orange and acrid smoke as the cottage was completely consumed by the fire.

It was around 4:30 am when a farmer planning to make an early start in the fields noticed the glow coming from the direction of the cottage. At first, he thought it was a bonfire, perhaps someone burning debris. But as he approached, the glow grew brighter and more intense, and the farmer's heart raced as he realised what was happening. He quickly called the emergency services, his voice shaking as he reported the fire.

Within minutes, the distant sound of sirens getting ever closer pierced the night air as fire engines raced to the scene, their lights flashing urgently. The fire had taken hold of the cottage with a terrifying speed, feeding on the old wooden beams and dry thatch that made up much of the building. The firefighters, used to this sort of fire in old Devon buildings, immediately began their work, but it was clear that they were fighting a losing battle. The cottage was engulfed in flames, the heat so intense that it was impossible to get too close.

By the time the fire was finally under control, the damage was catastrophic, and even when the fire was put out, the remaining wooden frame smouldered for the next few hours. The entire structure had collapsed in on itself, leaving nothing but steaming ruins and ash. The firefighters, now exhausted and covered in soot, stood back and surveyed the scene with heavy hearts. They knew that what had once been a charming, historic cottage was no more.

DS Saxon Brooks had been deeply asleep when the call came in, and yet he was still among the first on the scene once the fire had been subdued. He arrived just as the first light of dawn began to creep over the horizon, casting a pale glow on the devastation. This was no ordinary house fire; this was Dr Merton's home, the epicentre of a case that had once again grown more complicated to unravel.

Brooks stepped out of his car and surveyed the scene, his sharp eyes taking in every detail. The air was thick with the acrid smell of burnt wood and chemicals, and the ground was slick with water from the fire hoses. He approached the fire watch manager, a burly man with a weathered face, who was directing the final stages of the cleanup.

"Chief," Brooks greeted him, his voice steady despite the churn of unease in his gut. "What's the situation?"

The officer sighed, wiping sweat from his brow despite the cool morning air. "It's bad. The whole place is gone. We managed to stop it from spreading to the surrounding trees and buildings, but the cottage itself...there's nothing left."

Brooks nodded, ready with his next question. "Any idea what caused it? Was it an accident, or do we have reason to suspect foul play?"

The chief hesitated, glancing back at the smouldering remains of the cottage. "It's too early to say for sure. We'll need to conduct a thorough investigation once the site cools down, but I'll tell you this: it's suspicious. The fire spread too quickly, too intensely for there not to have been an accelerant involved. Could be an accident, but I've seen fires like this before, and they don't usually start spontaneously."

Brooks's jaw tightened. The idea of arson sent a chill down his spine, but it wasn't entirely unexpected. Dr Merton's death had been shrouded in mystery, and this could be someone determined to keep it that way.

"Right," said Brooks, "I'll need to have a look around, see if there's anything left that could give us a clue. This is the home of the victim in a murder investigation."

The chief nodded. "Be careful, though. It's still dangerous. The remaining structure's unstable, and there could be hot spots we haven't found yet."

Brooks thanked the chief and approached the ruins with cautious steps, still feeling the remnants of the heat hanging in the air. The cottage had been reduced to a blackened pile of debris, the once cosy home now unrecognisable. As he picked his way through the still-hot wreckage, he tried to piece together what might have happened.

So far, the investigation into Dr Merton's death had uncovered far more questions than answers, and now this fire had potentially erased vital evidence that could have unlocked the mystery. If it was arson, the question was who would go to such lengths to destroy the cottage. Was there something inside the cottage that someone wanted to hide? Or was it a message, a warning to those who were getting too close to the truth?

Brooks's thoughts were interrupted by the arrival of DI Barton along with Pip. They had been alerted to the fire when they were out on a very early walk, and Barton had brought Pip with him rather than disturb Lydia. They joined Brooks at the edge of the wreckage, his eyes scanning the scene with a sense of frustration.

"Bloody hell," Barton muttered, his voice thick with disbelief. "I thought we were done with surprises in this case, but this…"

Brooks shook his head. "It's like something out of a nightmare. We're going to have to go through this place with a fine-tooth comb, see if there's anything left that can give us a clue."

Barton nodded, his mind already racing through the possibilities. "We'll need to bring in forensics, get the fire investigation team on this as soon as possible. If it's arson, we need to know how it was done, and more importantly, who did it."

As the two detectives stood in the early morning light, the enormity of the task ahead. The fire had destroyed more than just a building; it had made the investigation much more difficult.

"Thank God, we took those papers, notebooks, and USB drive away – at least we still have something to go on. We should keep the fact that we have those to just you, me and Miranda, it will buy us time to make sense of the research," said Brooks.

One of the investigators, Lucy Hawthorn, had been sifting through the debris and approached the detectives. She had a grim expression, her face smudged with ash and soot.

"It's too early to give a definitive answer," she began, "but I can tell you that this fire didn't start naturally. There is evidence of an accelerant used to make sure this place went up fast and hot. It's on the ground all the way around the cottage. This wasn't just a random act of violence; this was deliberate, calculated, and meant to leave nothing behind."

Barton frowned. "Arson, then?"

Hawthorn nodded. "That's the most likely scenario. We'll need to analyse samples to be certain, but based on what I've seen so far, I'd say someone wanted this place gone in a hurry."

Brooks exchanged a glance with Barton, the implications of Hawthorn's words sinking in. "Is there anything left that could be of use to us?" Brooks asked, his voice tinged with urgency.

Hawthorn hesitated. "Most of it is destroyed, but we're doing our best. There are a few areas that weren't quite as heavily damaged, some of the floorboards in the back room, for example. We might be able to recover something from there, but really, I wouldn't hold my breath. Also, there have been two cats hanging around. I think they must have been Dr Merton's, the way they are prowling around the garden. I spoke to one of the neighbours who has been feeding them, and they seemed to have moved in. They have definitely both used up a life each, avoiding being caught up in that fire."

Barton nodded grimly. "Do what you can; every scrap of information counts."

Then he looked round and noticed Pip had left his side. As Hawthorn returned to her team, he saw Pip walking by her side. Brooks turned to Barton. "This fire wasn't just about destroying the cottage; it was about silencing whatever secrets Dr Merton was keeping."

Barton's jaw clenched. "It means we're getting closer to something someone doesn't want us to find. We need to keep the pressure on, follow every lead, no matter how small. How is the decrypting going on the files and the cottage USB, Saxon?"

"Could be, I think I will have at least some files available by the end of the day."

Barton was just about to call for Pip to come, so he and Brooks could get back to the station, when Lucy called them back: she was holding something small and delicate in her gloved hand.

"Detectives," she said, with a smile, "Pip has found something. It's a bit of a miracle it survived the fire, we may not have noticed it ourselves, but he was having a good scrabble around in the cooler wet mud at the back of the cottage."

Pip stood with his tail wagging vigorously, his muzzle and paws no longer their usual golden colour, but covered in a sticky black mixture of mud and soot. He seemed so proud of himself; it was as if he knew he had cracked the case.

Lucy handed the object to Brooks, who took it carefully, his eyes narrowing as he examined it. It was a small metal box, heavily scorched but still intact. The box was sealed, and whatever was inside had possibly been protected from the flames."

Barton leaned in, curious. "What do you think it is?"

Brooks shook his head. "I'm not sure, but whatever it is, it must have been important enough to keep it hidden like that. We need to get this back to the station, see if we can open it without damaging what's inside."

With the box safely secured, Brooks and Barton left the scene and headed back to the station, dropping Pip off on the way. Lydia was going to have an afternoon of bathing their beloved dog.

The fire had been a devastating blow to their investigation, but the discovery of the metal box felt like a phoenix rising from the ashes. Whatever secrets Evelyn Merton had been keeping, they were now one step closer to uncovering them. Once back at the station, Brooks and Barton sat in a small, secure room, the metal box placed carefully on the table between them. They had called in an expert to help with the delicate task of opening the box, someone who could ensure that whatever was inside would be preserved.

The expert, a forensic scientist named Neil Marshall, arrived shortly after them. He was a strange and solitary man who had once been with the bomb squad, known for his steady hands and obsessive attention to detail. After carefully examining the box, he nodded to the detectives.

"It's a challenge, but I think I can open it without causing any damage. I'll need some time, though," Marshall said in his soft Edinburgh accent.

Brooks and Barton watched as Marshall set to work using a variety of tools to carefully pry open the box's lid. The room was silent, the tension unbearable as the minutes ticked by. Finally, after what felt like an eternity, there was a soft click, and the lid popped open.

Marshall theatrically stepped back like a magician having pulled a rabbit from his hat, allowing Brooks and Barton to peer inside. The contents of the box were surprising: a stack of Post-it notes, slightly singed around the edges but otherwise intact, and a small, cheap notebook.

Brooks reached in and gingerly lifted the Post-it notes out, peeling them apart and spreading them on the table. The writing was faded but legible, and as he scanned the pages, his eyes widened.

"Barton," he said, his voice tinged with disbelief, "some of these are just more handwritten notes about Dr Merton's research, but this bundle all seem to be malicious attacks on Dr Merton's character. These typed letters are very threatening. I wonder if these were what was making her feel paranoid." Brooks continued, picking up the notebook, "…this looks like a journal. Maybe it'll give us more insight into what she was working on, and perhaps why someone wanted her silenced."

The two detectives sat in the small room for hours, poring over the contents of the box. The more they read, the clearer it became that Evelyn Merton's research appeared to have uncovered something that could have far-reaching consequences. It also became clear that they were dealing with a dangerous adversary, someone who was willing to threaten to protect their secrets. The fire had been a warning, but it had also revealed a crucial piece of the puzzle.

As the day moved into evening, Brooks and Barton felt that they were on the brink of a breakthrough. The fire had destroyed the cottage, but it had also exposed the desperation of whoever was trying to cover up the truth. Now, with the contents of the metal box in their possession, they were closer than ever to uncovering the secrets that had cost Evelyn Merton her life. Brooks and Barton needed to piece together the final elements of the puzzle before their adversary could make another move.

As they wearily prepared to leave the station, Barton turned to Brooks. "We're getting close, Saxon. But whoever did this is dangerous, and they won't hesitate to come after us if they think we're onto them."

With the metal box securely locked in the evidence room, Brooks and Barton set out into the night. The fire at the cottage had revealed the lengths to which their adversary was willing to go to keep their secrets hidden. Now Barton had to discover how Lydia's cleaning operation on Pip had gone.

Chapter 17

Barton sat in his office, tapping a pen rhythmically against the worn wood of his desk. Outside the room was filling with the quiet hum of the start of the day's activities, officers moving in and out with reports. Barton was oblivious to any of these distractions; he was preoccupied with the tangled threads of the case surrounding Dr Merton's death. The fire at her cottage had complicated matters, but what gnawed at him most was the mystery of what Dr Merton had been working on before her untimely demise; he couldn't yet piece it all together. He collected up his thoughts, notes and any evidence he considered relevant and made his way to his car for the drive up to Oxford.

He had spent the previous day combing through the papers, letters and journals recovered from the cottage and Dr Merton's office. What information he had extracted was so fragmented, it was like trying to read the few pages of a book without knowing what came before or indeed after. The clues pointed to an obscure medieval manuscript, but its significance was shrouded in mystery. This morning, Barton had received a call that might help shed light on this aspect of the case: the offer of a meeting with Professor Lowman.

Lowman worked in the same era as Dr Merton, and Barton hoped that the professor could provide some much-needed context. The thought of meeting Lowman, an academic heavyweight, left Barton feeling slightly uneasy. He was accustomed to dealing with criminals and witnesses, not erudite scholars. But this case had pulled him into a world far removed from his usual fare.

As Barton drove through the picturesque streets of Oxford, his mind wandered to Henry Lowman's reputation. The professor was known for his expertise in medieval manuscripts, particularly those shrouded in mystery and controversy. If anyone cast light on Evelyn Merton's research, it would be him.

Oxford was a maze of ancient stone buildings and colleges, ivy-clad walls and cobblestone paths. Barton parked his car in the Garden Quad at Balliol College and was shown to the history department through a maze of corridors to Lowman's office. The corridors were lined with portraits of distinguished academics from across the ages, their stern faces seeming to judge the detective as he passed by. Finally, Barton found himself standing before a heavy oak door with a brass nameplate that read, "Dr Henry Lowman, Professor of Medieval History."

Taking a deep breath, Barton knocked on the door; it creaked open almost immediately. A thin, bespectacled man in his early sixties, with thinning grey hair and a patched jacket that looked as old as the building, stood in the doorway. He had an air of absent-minded brilliance, the kind that one might expect from a man who spent his life immersed in the world of medieval Europe.

"Detective Barton, I presume?" Lowman's voice was soft, cultured and carried the faintest trace of an Oxfordshire dialect.

"Yes, that's right. Thank you for agreeing to meet with me, Professor Lowman," Barton replied, extending his hand.

Lowman shook it warmly and gestured for Barton to enter. "Michael Dixon speaks very highly of you, Detective Inspector Barton." The office was a scholar's sanctuary; everywhere the eye could see, there were ancient texts, manuscripts and journals. A large desk dominated the room, cluttered with papers, open books and a half-eaten sandwich, suggesting that the professor's dedication to his work often overshadowed mundane tasks like eating. There was a distinct similarity between Dr Merton's cottage and this office.

"Please, have a seat," Lowman offered, moving a stack of books from a chair so Barton could sit down. "I understand you're here about Dr Evelyn Merton. Tragic business, that. She had a brilliant mind, truly one of a kind."

Barton nodded, taking the seat. "Yes, the investigation is complicated, and the more we uncover, the less we seem to know. I was hoping you could help shed some light on her work, specifically, the manuscript she was researching."

Lowman leaned back in his chair, steepling his fingers as he considered Barton's request "Evelyn and I have occasionally corresponded over the years since she left Balliol, exchanging ideas and thoughts on various medieval texts. She was particularly interested in manuscripts that were lost or incomplete, those with gaps in their provenance. You see, she believed that these texts could hold the key to understanding aspects of medieval history that have remained obscure or misunderstood."

"What can you tell me about this particular manuscript?" Barton asked, his pen poised to take notes.

Lowman frowned slightly, as if dredging up a memory. "From what I gather, Evelyn was focused on a manuscript known as the '*Vita Regis,* ' which roughly translates as '*The Life of the King.*' Rumours of its existence started around eleven or twelve years ago and, since then, have been shrouded in controversy, even doubts as to whether it ever existed as one manuscript. It appears that Evelyn felt she had evidence that it really did exist There is a more well-known document called *Vita Ædwardi Regis* but that was about Edward the Confessor; the *Vita Regis* Evelyn was looking for was thought to be a 12th-century text, supposedly written by a monk who was close to the court of an English king, though which king remains a matter of quite vigorous debate. The manuscript is controversial because it tells stories that challenge the established narratives of the time."

Barton leaned forward, intrigued. "How so?"

"Well, the *Vita Regis* is said to contain accounts of events that never made it into the official chronicles. A strange mythology has grown around it. Some historians believe it references a hidden council, a group of powerful nobles who effectively controlled the monarchy from behind the scenes. Others suggest it might include evidence of forgotten battles or treaties that could change our understanding of medieval politics."

"So, it's more than just an old book," Barton said, scribbling down notes. "It's potentially explosive."

"Indeed, it would be, if proven," Lowman agreed, a glint of excitement in his eyes. "If the contents of the manuscript were to be fully authenticated and understood, it could reshape our understanding of that whole period and possibly beyond. But there's a catch: the manuscript is fragmented. Parts of it are missing, and its authenticity has been questioned by many scholars. Some think it's a forgery or even a hoax, others that the missing sections were intentionally destroyed to hide the truth."

Barton absorbed this information, his mind racing with the implications. "Do you think Dr Merton had found something that could prove the manuscript's authenticity or reveal its true contents?"

Lowman hesitated, choosing his words carefully. "Evelyn was always very secretive about her research. I got the sense that she felt she was onto something significant, but she didn't share many details with me. When she wrote to me a few months ago, she said that she had been working with a private collector, a wealthy individual who had acquired some rare medieval texts. It's possible that she had come across new evidence, something that could verify the *Vita Regis* or even restore the missing parts."

"A private collector?" Barton echoed, feeling a familiar knot of tension forming.

"Do you have any idea who this might be?"

Lowman shook his head slowly. "She didn't mention the name, and I didn't press her for it. Academics sometimes want to keep their sources a secret until publication, especially when dealing with valuable or controversial material."

Barton suppressed a sigh. Another dead end, or so it seemed. But the mention of a private collector had been raised before in this case. Perhaps this collector had a role in Merton's death, or maybe they were simply a key to understanding what had driven her to take such risks with her research.

"Do you think her work could have put her in danger?" Barton asked, probing further.

Lowman looked pensive, his thoughts evident in the lines of his face. "It's possible, although somewhat unlikely. The academic world can be fiercely competitive, and when you're dealing with something as potentially revolutionary as the *Vita Regis*, there are always those who would go to great lengths to protect their reputations and theories, or even their financial interests. Evelyn wasn't one to back down, even if it meant crossing powerful individuals."

"Powerful individuals?" Barton pressed. "Are we talking about people within the academic community, or could it be someone outside of it?"

Lowman sighed, rubbing the bridge of his nose. "Both, I'm afraid. There are wealthy patrons of the arts and history who have a vested interest in certain narratives remaining unchallenged. Within academia, there are those whose entire careers and reputations are built on the established interpretations of history. If Evelyn had evidence that could undermine that, she could have made enemies, although I have never been aware of any."

Barton was trying to piece together the puzzle with this new information. "Professor, do you think Evelyn might have shared her findings with anyone else? Colleagues, friends, maybe someone who could verify her work?"

Lowman shook his head. "Not to my knowledge. As I said, she always kept things very close to her chest. If she did confide in anyone, it would have been someone she trusted implicitly. Evelyn wasn't one to share unfinished work lightly."

The detective leaned back in his chair, thoughts whirling about his head. "What about her assistant, Miranda Jackson? Could she have known more than she let on?"

"Miranda?" Lowman mused. "From what Evelyn said in her letter, she sounds like a highly capable young woman. Evelyn spoke highly of her abilities, though I am not sure how close they were outside of their professional relationship. If Evelyn was working on something critical, Miranda might well have been involved in some capacity, but it's hard to say how much detail she would have known."

Barton nodded, making a note to re-examine his conversations with Miranda. Perhaps there were clues there that he had overlooked. "Professor, one last question: do you have any idea what Evelyn's next steps might have been? If she had uncovered something important, where would she have gone from there?"

Lowman thought for a moment, his brow furrowed in concentration. "If Evelyn had found something definitive, she would have been preparing a paper or a presentation for one of the major medieval history conferences. But knowing her, she would have wanted to verify and cross-check her findings thoroughly before making any public announcement. It's possible she was planning to consult with other scholars discreetly."

Barton thanked Lowman for his time and insight, feeling

that he had gained valuable context for understanding Dr Merton's research and the potential dangers it posed. As he walked out of the history department, his mind was churning with new possibilities and new avenues to pursue. If Evelyn Merton had been on the brink of something monumental, could that something have cost her life?

Back in his car, Barton sat for a moment, reflecting on the conversation. He knew that the next step would be to trace Evelyn's connections to this elusive manuscript and the mysterious collector.

As he started the drive back to Exeter, Barton's thoughts turned to his next move. He needed to find out who else might have known about it, because if Evelyn Merton had been killed to keep a secret, that secret was still out there, waiting to be discovered. He had a thought and called Brooks.

"OK, prioritise the cottage USB over everything else – it is more likely to be Dr Merton's." He knew that Saxon's tech pride would have been dented by the fake "Ha, Ha, Ha" disk, and that would make him redouble his efforts.

When he got off the phone, Barton cursed – this investigation was just going round in circles. When he got home, he and Pip were going to go on a very long walk so Barton could digest all that had happened while they walked by the river as it gently flowed past them, as it had done for thousands of years. Pip would amble along being the perfect silent companion, not questioning, just being there.

Chapter 18

Lydia had spent the day cleaning; she had always prided herself on being a woman of routine and order, traits that had served her well throughout her personal and professional life. While her husband grappled with the often chaotic and dark world of crime and investigation, Lydia found solace in the structure and the predictable rhythm of her days, and in the quiet rituals that punctuated her life alongside the framework of her historical research. With the death of her friend, her research had ground to a halt; she just couldn't face it for now, although she had an idea about that. However, until she could put that in place, she threw herself into her annual spring cleaning, only four months late this year. She had been shattered to hear about the arson attack on Evelyn's cottage; the two women had shared so many happy times. It gave her cleaning extra vigour, even though she would never be able to explain why.

The day had started like any other. Lydia had set about her task with her usual efficiency, dusting and polishing, sorting and organising. The warm sunlight filtered through the curtains, casting a gentle glow over the room as she moved from one task to the next. It was in the process of clearing out her wardrobe in their bedroom, sorting through the contents, that she found it, a small, unassuming parcel wrapped in plain brown paper.

At first, she didn't recognise it. She turned it over in her hands, feeling the weight of it, trying to recall where it had come from. Then, slowly, the memory returned. It had been quite a few years ago, Evelyn had, unusually, come to Lydia's house one evening, probably the first and only time she had been there, looking unusually serious. She had handed Lydia the parcel with a request that seemed odd at the time. Evelyn had asked Lydia to keep it safe, to tuck it away somewhere out of sight, and to forget about it until she was told otherwise. Then, rather than coming in for a chat as you would expect from a friend, she headed off into the darkness, promising to be in touch soon as she disappeared into the night.

Lydia had agreed, of course, trusting Evelyn implicitly, though she hadn't ever given much thought to what might be inside. After all, Evelyn was a historian, constantly dealing with ancient documents and obscure artefacts. Lydia had assumed it was something of little consequence, at least in her world.

Now, as she held the parcel in her hands, Lydia felt a growing sense of unease. The recent conversations with Whipton about Evelyn's death, the mysterious manuscript, and the potential dangers surrounding her research suddenly came rushing back. Could this parcel have something to do with all of that? Could it hold a clue, perhaps even the key, to understanding what had happened to her friend? Could she have been the person Professor Lowman had referred to in his conversation with Whipton, as a close friend and confidante?

The more she thought about it, the more certain she became that she needed to show it to Whipton. He would know what to do.

Lydia set the parcel aside on the bed, finishing her cleaning. Her thoughts were consumed with what might be inside, but she forced herself to stay focused, knowing that Whipton would soon be back. When he had arrived home early, he had gone straight out again to take Pip on a longer-than-usual walk and think about the case before she even had the chance to show him the parcel. This walk would help calm him down after the long days at work, and on their return, Pip would slump into a deep and contented sleep with his family around him.

When Barton finally walked through the door that evening, he was greeted with the familiar, comforting sight of their home, spotless and well-organised, just as Lydia had always kept it. But there was something different in the air, a tension that Barton picked up on immediately. Pip had his usual vigorous drink from his bowl, picked up his favourite toy and headed for his basket. Lydia caught Whipton looking somewhat enviously at the simple, yet joyous, life that a happy dog could live.

Whipton looked up "Everything alright, Lyd?" he asked, noticing the look of concern on her face.

She nodded, but her expression remained serious. "Whip, there's something I need to show you that I found today."

Barton followed her upstairs to the bedroom, where Lydia handed him the parcel she had found. He turned it over in his hands, his brow furrowing as he examined it.

"Evelyn gave this to me a few years ago," Lydia explained. "She asked me to keep it safe. I put it away and had completely forgotten about it. I just did as she asked. I have been cleaning all day, and I came across it again at the back of my wardrobe. When I found it, I could have kicked myself, with everything you've been telling me about her research, about that manuscript…I think maybe this is important."

Barton sat on the bed and carefully unwrapped the parcel, revealing a small, cardboard box. Inside, nestled in soft, old linen, was a collection of documents, some of them yellowed with age, others more recent, neatly typed on crisp paper.

As Barton sifted through the contents, he realised that these weren't just any documents. They were research notes, drafts, all related to the mysterious *Vita Regis* that Professor Lowman had said Evelyn had been investigating.

"This is…incredible," Barton murmured, his eyes scanning the delicate pages. "These look like Evelyn's notes on the manuscript she was working on. But there's more here, look at this."

He held up a particularly old, fragile piece of parchment, covered in intricate early Gothic script. He guessed it was a passage from the *Vita Regis*, written in a hand that seemed ancient even by medieval standards. The text was dense and in Latin, but Barton guessed it may be significant immediately.

"This could be a missing piece," Barton said, his voice filled with a mix of excitement and trepidation. "This could be what Evelyn was using to try to prove the authenticity of this manuscript. Thank God she gave it to you; this would never have survived the fire."

Lydia watched as her husband carefully examined each document, his expression growing more intense with each discovery. She could see him gradually piecing the puzzle together.

But there was something else in the box, something that caught Barton's attention. Beneath the layers of paper, hidden at the very bottom, was another journal, the pages yellowed with age.

Barton opened the notebook, flipping through the pages. It was a diary detailing Evelyn's thoughts and experiences as she delved deeper into her research. As he read, Barton's expression darkened.

"There's something here," he said, his voice low. "Something she was afraid of. She mentions receiving threats, letters, and phone calls."

Lydia felt a chill run down her spine. "Do you think that's why she gave this to me? Because she was afraid?"

"It's possible, it would mean she has been afraid for quite a long time," Barton replied. "She must have known she was onto something that someone didn't want her to uncover. If that's the case, then this parcel could be the most important piece of evidence so far."

As they continued to go through the contents of the box, they found more of Evelyn's notes that pointed to the significance of the *Vita Regis*. There were references to a shadowy group of nobles who had manipulated the monarchy from behind the scenes, a group that had been erased from the official history books. Evelyn had been piecing together their existence, connecting the dots that others had missed. There was more evidence that this group had left a legacy that stretched into the present day. Evelyn had been tracing their influence through the centuries, uncovering connections to modern-day figures and institutions. If it were real, it would indeed be a historical time bomb if it were ever made public. If Evelyn had been close to exposing a secret that had been buried for centuries. And that could be why she had been killed.

"This is bigger than I thought," Barton said. "It looks as though Evelyn was on the verge of uncovering something that could change the way we understand history, and this is as close as we have got to a possible motive."

Lydia felt a surge of fear. "What are we going to do, Whip?"

Barton placed a reassuring hand on her shoulder. "We'll be careful. I'll take this to the station, make sure it's secured as evidence."

Lydia nodded, trusting in her husband's words, but a germ of fear remained. As Barton gathered the documents and prepared to take them to his study, she couldn't shake the feeling that they were now caught up in something far beyond their control.

That night, as Barton sat in his study, poring over the documents, the *Vita Regis* wasn't just a manuscript; it must be the key to understanding a hidden history, one that had been carefully concealed for centuries – and Evelyn had been on the brink of exposing it all.

As he worked late into the night, his mind raced with possibilities. The clues were there, hidden in the ancient texts and Evelyn's notes. He knew that he would have to tread carefully: one wrong move, and the truth may remain buried forever.

When he got to the station the next morning, Barton briefed his team on the discovery. They would need to follow the leads that he had found in Evelyn's notes, track down the people she had been in contact with, and find out if anyone knew who had been threatening her.

As he left the station, Brooks stopped him. "You were right, the USB and encrypted documents we took away from the cottage are authentic, and they have added a bit more to the story than you found in Lydia's package. It implies a council of power that controls the monarch and government, maintaining its power and keeping the general public in blissful ignorance. I am so glad the cottage USB had something, I thought I was losing my touch!"

Chapter 19

Miranda Jackson sat at the small wooden desk and surveyed her modest apartment. The afternoon sun was struggling to get through the clouds, and so the flat had become quite dark. To help Barton, she had spent the better part of the week poring over documents, cross-referencing names, dates and notes from Evelyn's office and cottage, all in an attempt to uncover something, anything, that might shed light on Dr Merton's death. There were papers arranged in meticulous order on the desk and every other surface in the room, including the floor. While working on this, she had also been worried about what her job would be now, how she was going to make a living. It seemed cold, but it was also a cruel, hard fact of life that bills still have to be paid.

It wasn't just the shock of her boss's death that drove her, but also the unsettling feeling that something hadn't been right in the weeks leading up to it. Evelyn had been more secretive than usual, more guarded. Miranda had noticed it, but at the time, she had attributed it to the pressures of their work. Now she wasn't so sure.

Miranda had greatly admired Evelyn, which made the loss all the more painful. Then there was Edward Voss, a person who had started to haunt her thoughts since they met. Could he have a connection to Evelyn's death?

Miranda had seen Evelyn like her academic mother, guiding her through the complexities of research and the politics of university life. When she had been offered the position as Evelyn's assistant, she had felt honoured, and in the past three months, it had become clear that Evelyn was also her mentor. That was why, when her behaviour had started to change, Miranda had noticed it immediately. The first hint of something amiss had come during one of their routine meetings about the latest research. Evelyn had been distracted, her eyes darting to the window, her responses curt and distant. Miranda had asked if something was wrong, but Evelyn had attributed her mood to the stress of her project. Now Miranda couldn't shake the feeling that it was something else.

After Evelyn's death, Miranda had become obsessed with finding out what had happened. She had initially assumed that it had been a tragic accident or perhaps the result of some underlying health issue that Evelyn had kept hidden. As the days passed, the increasing number of connections to Edward Voss and too many strange coincidences, too many unanswered questions in the police investigation kept going round in her head.

Now Miranda decided to take matters into her own hands, do what she did best, research. She knew that Voss had been Evelyn's assistant immediately before Miranda, although admittedly, there had been a ten-year gap between them. Voss had apparently been brilliant, intelligent, creative and dedicated. But there had been something else in Evelyn's tone on the rare occasions she mentioned him, something Miranda had never been able to place. It wasn't just respect; there was an edge to it, a tension that seemed at odds with the high praise she offered.

Miranda had always assumed that Voss had left on good terms, that he had simply moved on to another position or another research project. But now, as she stared at his name on the list, she wondered if there was more to the story. Evelyn had never been one to gossip about her former assistants, but the way she had spoken about Voss suggested his time as her assistant had been more complicated than she had let on.

Miranda began digging deeper, looking for any information she could find on Voss. The university's records showed that he had left abruptly, his resignation letter terse and to the point. There were no details, no explanations, just a short note saying that he was resigning from his position as Evelyn's assistant effective immediately. It was unusual, to say the least, especially given the importance of the work they had been doing at the time. There was also no evidence that he had even been given a reference by Evelyn.

Why had Dr Merton gone without an assistant for so long? The more she thought about it, the more it seemed that Voss's departure had not been as smooth as she had originally assumed.

Miranda's next step was to look online into Voss's career after he left Evelyn's employment. She found that he had taken a position at another university, but there were gaps in his resumé, periods where he seemed to vanish from the academic world altogether. There were rumours, too, whispers of a falling out with a colleague, of a research project that had ended in disaster. Nothing concrete, but enough to make Miranda wonder what had happened. Miranda started to piece together a picture of a man who was at once both brilliant and volatile, someone who could be charming and persuasive but also ruthless when it came to his work. Voss seemed to have a pattern of intense involvement in short-lived projects, always featuring sudden departures when things didn't go his way. It was as if he shone bright and then burnt out like a match, leaving chaos in his wake. Then he seemed to leave academia completely when he met the socialite Victoria Berger. The couple appeared in many editions of the glossy county-set magazine for about a year, and then there was coverage of the engagement and wedding. Then they seemed to disappear for a while until he opened his shop on Cathedral Green, rumoured to have been funded by the Berger family.

Miranda's research led her to speak with some of Evelyn's former colleagues, people who had known her during the time she worked with Voss. Most of them were reluctant to talk, offering only vague platitudes about the difficulties of academic life. But one professor was more forthcoming. He described Voss as brilliant but difficult to work with, someone who pushed boundaries and wasn't afraid to challenge authority.

"He and Evelyn clashed a lot," the professor said, his voice low as if he feared being overheard. "They were both strong personalities, both driven by their work. But Voss had a shadier side. He was ambitious to the point of obsession. I remember hearing about some heated arguments between them, particularly towards the end. I wasn't surprised when he left, but in the way he left, so suddenly, it raised a lot of eyebrows."

Miranda pressed him for more details, but the professor seemed reluctant to say anything further. "Look," he said finally, "academia is a small world. People talk, but it's mostly speculation. Whatever happened between Edward and Evelyn, it's in the past now. But if you're looking for answers, you might want to be careful. There are things that are better left buried."

The warning sent a chill down Miranda's spine; she was convinced now that Voss had something to do with Evelyn's death, even if she didn't know exactly what. The connection between them was too strong, too fraught with tension to be a coincidence.

Miranda decided to confront the situation head-on. She reached out to HR again, this time requesting any records of complaints or incidents involving Voss during his time at the university. It took some persuasion, but eventually, she was able to access a file that showed a formal complaint Evelyn had filed against Voss shortly before his departure.

The complaint was vague, mentioning "unprofessional conduct" and "disagreements over research methods." But there was a note attached from the HR director at the time, stating that the matter had been resolved internally, with Voss agreeing to leave the position with immediate effect. The file didn't offer much more information, but it confirmed what Miranda had suspected: Voss and Evelyn's relationship had ended on bad terms.

Armed with this new information, Miranda knew she needed to take her findings to Barton. The detective had been thorough in his searches of Evelyn's office and cottage, but Miranda suspected that he hadn't been able to fully explore the Voss angle. She hoped that her research would help him see the bigger picture, that it would point him towards the truth about Evelyn's death.

Before she could go to Barton, Miranda felt she wanted to speak to Voss directly, and after some hesitation, she decided to drop a message into the shop after hours. Her message was simple: she wanted to ask him some questions about his time working with Evelyn, framing it as part of a retrospective project about her life and work. To her surprise, Voss called her and agreed to meet with her at a quiet café near the University the next day, a place where they could talk without being disturbed.

Miranda was nervous as she made her way to the café, unsure of what to expect. She had dressed in her favourite clothes, the ones that made her feel strong and able to take on the world. In her satchel, she had her list of questions, but she knew that the conversation could go in a number of directions, and she would have to be at her sharpest.

When she arrived at the café, she spotted Voss sitting at a table by the window. She recognised him immediately from the awkward visit to the shop with Lydia, his hair greying at the temples, but there was still a sharpness in his eyes, a quickness to his movements that spoke of a mind always at work. As she strode to the table, he greeted her with a short-lived polite smile, though there was coldness to his expression that made Miranda uneasy, that same sense of threat she had had at the shop.

They exchanged stiff pleasantries, and then Miranda began to ask her questions. Voss was guarded at first, offering only vague answers about his time working with Evelyn. He spoke in generalities, focusing on the positive aspects of their collaboration, but Miranda could sense that Voss had no respect for any women or their intellectual capacity. The more he spoke, the more condescending he became. Miranda decided to take a more direct approach. She mentioned the complaint Evelyn had filed, watching Voss's reaction carefully. For a moment, he stiffened, his smile fading. But then he recovered, dismissing the question with a wave of his hand.

"That was a long time ago," Voss said, his tone casual but with what felt like an underlying anger. "Evelyn and I had our disagreements, but that's common in academia. We were both passionate about our work, and sometimes that led to conflict. But it was nothing more than that, a clash of ideas, nothing personal."

Miranda wasn't convinced. She pressed further, asking about the suddenness of his departure, about the rumours she had heard from other colleagues. Voss's air grew colder, his answers shorter. It was clear that he didn't want to discuss the past, especially not the more contentious aspects of it.

Finally, Miranda decided to confront him with what she had found about his departure and Evelyn's complaint in his HR file. She watched as Voss's eyes narrowed as he realised where she was going with her line of questioning.

"You've done your homework, I see," Voss said, his voice low and measured. "But be careful, Miranda. Sometimes, digging too deep can lead to places you don't want to go."

There was an underlying threat in his words, but it was

unmistakable. Miranda felt a chill run through her, but she didn't back down. She had come too far.

"I'm just trying to understand what happened to Evelyn," Miranda said, keeping her voice steady. "If there's something you know, something that could help, I think you should tell me."

Voss leaned back in his chair, studying her for a long moment. Then he sighed, as if resigning himself to his starring role in the conversation.

"Evelyn was a brilliant woman," he said, his tone softer now, almost wistful. "But she was also stubborn, unwilling to compromise. Our work together was some of the most challenging I've ever done, but it was also some of the most rewarding. We pushed each other, sometimes too far."

He paused, his gaze drifting to the window. "There were things she didn't understand, things she wasn't ready to accept. And when I tried to make her see, she resisted. That's where our conflict came from, not personal animosity, but a difference in vision. In the end, I had to leave because I realised she would never see things my way."

Miranda listened, taking in Voss's every word. They seemed intentionally vague, something that had driven a wedge between him and Evelyn. She wondered what exactly it was that they had disagreed on, what 'vision' Voss had that Evelyn couldn't accept. Before she could ask, Voss stood up, signalling that the conversation was over. "I've said enough," he said, his tone final. "If you want to honour Evelyn's memory, I suggest you focus on the work she did, not the conflicts she had. Some things are better left in the past. The past is a shadow that shapes the present."

With that, Voss turned and walked out of the café, leaving Miranda sitting alone at the table. She watched him go, a mixture of frustration and determination boiling within her. She knew she was onto something, but she also knew that Voss wasn't going to give her the answers she needed willingly. As she gathered her things and prepared to leave, Miranda knew she had to give the information to DI Barton. Voss might be hiding something, but she wasn't going to let that stop her. Evelyn had trusted her, and she wasn't going to let her down.

Chapter 20

The initial postmortem examination had left a number of questions unanswered, but now with the toxicology report and some other screening, Barton would get a better picture of the crime itself. The full post-mortem report of Dr Evelyn Merton's body arrived at a critical juncture in the investigation. The peculiar circumstances surrounding her death had cast a shroud of mystery over the case, and the findings from the autopsy promised to provide much-needed clarity, or, as Barton feared, plunge them deeper into a labyrinth of questions.

The senior pathologist, Dr Katherine Fielding, was a brilliant young scientist and had taken over the investigation from Dr Jim, the duty pathologist who had conducted the initial examination. She was known for her unflinching attention to detail, and the report she produced was a typically comprehensive document, outlining every aspect of Dr Merton's physical state at the time of her death.

Dr Evelyn Merton was found in the Chapter House of Exeter Cathedral. The room had been locked at the end of the day, but unlocked when Thomas Jones came to open up the following day. How Dr Merton was found there in such an isolated, sacred space was a mystery, and more pressing, what and who had killed her?

The initial findings were consistent with a sudden, unexpected death. Dr Merton's body showed no external signs of trauma; there were no bruises, no lacerations, no defensive wounds and no signs of a struggle. The Chapter House itself had appeared undisturbed, suggesting that Dr Merton had not been moved after death. It was as if she had been lowered into place.

However, the first clue that something was amiss came from a closer examination of her fingernails. Dr Fielding noted that there were faint bluish discolouration at the tips, a telltale sign of cyanosis, indicating that Dr Merton had suffered from a lack of oxygen before she died. This finding pointed towards the possibility of poisoning, suffocation or some other form of asphyxiation.

Dr Fielding's initial examination revealed nothing conclusive, so she proceeded to dissect the heart, lungs and other vital organs. The lungs were congested, and there was evidence of pulmonary oedema, a fluid accumulation within the lung tissue. This pointed towards an acute event that had led to respiratory failure, but what had caused it was still unclear.

It wasn't until Dr Fielding reached the gastrointestinal tract that she found her next significant clue. The stomach's contents were sparse, suggesting that Dr Merton had not eaten for several hours before her death. However, the inner lining of her stomach and upper intestine showed signs of irritation, as though they had been exposed to a corrosive substance.

To confirm her suspicions, Dr Fielding sent samples to the toxicology lab for further analysis. The report continued with the autopsy, documenting her findings, but referring that the real answer lay in the toxicology report. The toxicology results came back after several days of anxious waiting. The lab had conducted a broad-spectrum screening analysis, testing for hundreds of potential poisons, drugs and toxins. The results were as chilling as they were illuminating. Dr Merton had been poisoned with a rare and deadly substance, aconitine.

"Aconitine is an alkaloid derived from the aconitum plant, commonly known as monkshood or wolfsbane. It is a potent neurotoxin, known for its ability to cause a rapid onset of a variety of possible symptoms, which could include severe hypertension, breathing difficulties, heart problems, and ultimately paralysis of the respiratory system. In small doses, it causes excruciating pain and nausea, and in larger doses, fatal heart or respiratory collapse. The presence of this quantity of aconitine in Dr Merton's system was conclusive evidence of the cause of death. The substance had been ingested, most likely in a liquid form, as suggested by the irritation found in her gastrointestinal tract. However, the dosage was so high that Dr Merton would have experienced severe symptoms within minutes, and death would have followed shortly thereafter." Dr Fielding explained.

The post-mortem and toxicology findings raised several crucial questions for Barton and his team. If Dr Merton had ingested the poison and died quickly in the Chapter House, why had there been no evidence of poison at the scene?

Dr Fielding's report offered a possible timeline. Based on the state of rigor mortis and other physiological markers, she agreed with the original assessment that Dr Merton had died approximately six to eight hours before her body was discovered. Given that she was found early in the morning, this placed her time of death between 10 pm and midnight the previous evening. Dr Fielding also noted that there was no evidence of post-mortem lividity, the pooling of blood in the body after death, which would suggest she had not been moved. The lividity patterns were consistent with her body having remained in the same position from the moment of death until discovery. This strongly indicated that Dr Merton had indeed died where she sat in the Chapter House.

But this conclusion only deepened the mystery. The Chapter House had been locked the previous evening, with no signs of forced entry or exit. How had Dr Merton ended up there, and how had the door been unlocked during the night?

The key to this puzzle lay in understanding the layout of the Chapter House and its history. The building was ancient, with many of its features dating back to the medieval period. The heavy wooden door was equipped with its original medieval lock, a complex mechanism that could only be operated by a large iron key. However, the door had been found unlocked – had it already been locked when Thomas Jackson had done his rounds the previous night, as he insisted it was? Or had he not remembered that the door was already locked? This would need to be checked with Thomas, as it was crucial to the timeline of that night.

This meant there were two options: Dr Merton either locked herself in – or someone else did. However, the key was with Thomas, and even if she was intent on suicide and had the key, she would have had to lock the door before ingesting the lethal dose of aconitine. But no key had been found at the scene, so it would seem that someone else must have been in the Chapter House as well.

This more sinister possibility was that Dr Merton had not been alone when she ingested the poison. What if someone else had been with her, someone she trusted? This person could have administered the poison, waited for her to die, and then unlocked the door from the inside before escaping into the Cathedral cloisters.

Barton and his team considered the possibilities. The first theory was that Dr Merton had taken the poison herself, intending to end her own life. She could have locked the door from the inside, then taken the aconitine in the Chapter House, and then succumbed to the poison. However, this theory didn't sit well with Barton. There was no evidence to suggest that Dr Merton had been suicidal. She had been engaged in her work, and from what Lydia and Miranda had said, she was looking forward to the completion of her research. More importantly, no poison had been found on any of her possessions at her table, and no key had been found in the Chapter House.

Another possibility was that the locked door was a deliberate ploy by the killer to mislead the investigators. But this would require the killer to have had intimate knowledge of the Cathedral routines, the Chapter House and its door's locking mechanism. Could the door have been unlocked from the inside in some way, or had the lock been manipulated to prevent it from fully locking that evening? This theory also had its flaws, particularly since there was no evidence of tampering with the lock.

Barton also considered the possibility that the poison had been administered in a way that delayed its effects, giving Dr Merton time to reach the Chapter House before the symptoms became incapacitating. Perhaps she had been poisoned earlier in the evening and had gone to the Chapter House either to seek solitude or to continue her work, unaware that she was dying. This theory was intriguing, but it hinged on the assumption that Dr Merton didn't realise she had been poisoned, something that seemed impossible, given the severity of symptoms and the quantity of aconitine in her body.

With all this in mind, Barton directed his team to conduct another thorough search of the Chapter House and the surrounding areas. They combed through every inch of the ancient structure, looking for any signs of someone being able to escape after locking the door from the inside. They also examined the door itself and Thomas's key, checking for any signs of tampering or unusual wear.

Their efforts were largely fruitless. The Chapter House was exactly what it appeared to be, a solitary, enclosed space. The door was solid, the lock functional, and the key showed no obvious signs of having been manipulated. The conclusion that Dr Merton had died in the Chapter House seemed inescapable, but the question of how she had ended up there remained maddeningly elusive.

Barton asked Dr Fielding to re-examine the toxicology results, focusing on the possibility that the aconitine had been administered in a way that slowed its absorption or delayed its effects. Dr Fielding acknowledged that aconitine could be absorbed through the skin or mucous membranes, potentially delaying the onset of symptoms, but the concentration found in Dr Merton's stomach suggested that she had ingested a large dose, which would have acted very quickly.

This led Barton to consider another angle: what if Dr Merton had ingested the poison unknowingly, thinking it was something else? Perhaps she had been given a drink or food laced with aconitine, unaware of its deadly contents. This would explain why she had not immediately sought help or attempted to escape; the poison could have been disguised as something innocuous.

To test this theory, Barton ordered a thorough examination of Dr Merton's belongings for any traces of aconitine or its source. The central question was whether had she taken it intentionally, or had someone else administered it?

Barton circled back to consider the possibility that Dr Merton had been involved in her own death, perhaps as part of a larger plan to protect her research or to prevent something she feared from coming to light. But this theory conflicted with everything Barton knew about her being committed to her work. Why would she kill herself when she was on the brink of a major discovery? The alternative was that someone else had poisoned her using aconitine, but if this was the case, who had the motive and opportunity to carry out such a plan?

One final possibility lingered in Barton's mind, unsettling in its implications: what if Dr Merton had been forced to take the poison? The locked room, no obvious receptacle for the poison, the lack of struggle, all pointed to a scenario in which she had ingested the aconitine without her knowledge. A chilling thought was that someone had planted the poison and had taken the evidence away with them after it had done its job.

Barton couldn't shake the feeling that the answers lay somewhere in Dr Merton's research, in the mysterious *Vita Regis* document she had been so obsessed with. Had her work uncovered something so dangerous that someone had resorted to murder to stop her? And if so, how far were they willing to go to keep the secrets buried?

With the post-mortem and toxicology reports in hand, Barton was closer to understanding the means of Dr Evelyn Merton's death, but there were still too many unanswered questions and no clear motive or suspect. The locked and then unlocked room, the aconitine, each piece of the puzzle led to more possibilities and more dead ends. He directed his team again to dig deeper into Dr Merton's research, her colleagues, and her personal life. Someone out there knew the truth, and Barton was determined to find them.

Chapter 21

The next stage was for Barton to delve into the physical evidence and the enigmatic world of academia while Brooks was working on the files from the USB retrieved from Dr Merton's cottage. There was still encryption, but it was far less sophisticated, as if it had been done by someone with only a basic knowledge of data security. Brooks had quickly decrypted the disc, and what he found inside was both illuminating and disturbing.

The cottage files contained a mixture of personal journals, correspondence and research notes. They offered a glimpse into Dr Merton's life beyond her academic persona: her thoughts, fears and the pressures she had been under in the months leading up to her death.

One file, labelled simply "Diary," was a collection of journal entries that revealed a more vulnerable side to Dr Merton. She wrote about her isolation, her struggles with her research and her growing suspicions. She mentioned feeling watched, followed and even sabotaged. There were cryptic references to someone she referred to only as "E," whom she described as both a collaborator and a threat.

In one particularly troubling entry, dated just weeks before her death, Dr Merton wrote:

"E has sent a message, he wants access to everything, my notes, my drafts, even the fragments. I can't let him have them, not after everything I've worked for. But how much longer can I keep this up? The pressure is unbearable. I fear what might happen if I say no."

Another subfolder contained correspondence between Dr Merton and various colleagues, some of which referenced the *Vita Regis* manuscript fragments. These fragments were ancient and incredibly valuable, believed to hold secrets about a long-lost king, his reign and the real power behind the throne. Dr Merton's research was focused on piecing together the history from these fragments, but it was clear from her correspondence that she was facing significant opposition.

One email, in particular, stood out. It was from an anonymous sender with an untraceable email account, and it simply read:

"You're getting too close. Stop now, or there will be consequences."

This warning was followed by a series of increasingly threatening messages, each more menacing than the last. Dr Merton had believed that she had been under immense scrutiny, not just from the academic community but from unknown forces who wanted to keep her from uncovering the truth.

As Brooks sifted through the files, it became apparent that Dr Merton's research into the *Vita Regis* fragments was at the heart of her project. The fragments were more than just historical curiosities; they were pieces of a puzzle that, if solved, could rewrite history.

One of the decrypted files was her detailed analysis of some of the fragments. She had identified several key pieces of information that hinted at a hidden lineage, a royal bloodline that had been erased from history. This lineage, if proven, could have serious implications, potentially challenging the legitimacy of the current British monarchy.

The files also appeared to reveal that Dr Merton had uncovered evidence of a cover-up, ancient documents that had been deliberately altered or destroyed to hide the truth.

She had traced this cover-up back to the medieval period, but there were indications that the suppression of information had continued into modern times.

Brooks found a particularly chilling note stuck: "They've been watching me since I found the last fragment. They know I'm close. If something happens to me, the truth must come out. The world needs to know."

It was clear that Dr Merton had feared for her life. She had taken precautions, encrypting her files and hiding her research, but in the end, it hadn't been enough – someone had silenced her.

Further on in the diary, Brooks found a more intimate insight into Dr Merton's thoughts, chronicling her day-to-day life. She wrote about her research, her interactions with colleagues, and the mounting pressure she felt as she delved deeper into the secrets of the *Vita Regis*.

One of the most striking entries in the journal was dated just a few days before her death: "I've been receiving more threats. They're becoming more specific, more personal. Someone knows what I'm working on, and they're getting desperate. I've tried to keep everything hidden, but I'm running out of places to turn. I don't know who I can trust anymore. If they get their hands on the fragments, it will all have been for nothing. I have to find a way to protect them, even if it means destroying everything."

Brooks noted that Dr Merton referred to "E" more frequently in her journal, but she never mentioned a full name. This could be Edward Voss. When Brooks briefed Barton, he couldn't ignore that possibility, especially given what else he had uncovered in the digital files.

As Barton read the journal, he noticed it contained several cryptic references to a "final piece" of the puzzle, something that Dr Merton had been searching for but had not yet found. She wrote about needing to return to a specific location, a place she referred to only as "the Source," to find this missing piece. Barton had no idea what or who "the Source" referred to, but it was clear that Dr Merton believed it held the key to everything.

When Brooks and Barton compared the evidence so far, there were some connections and some deliberate misdirection. The encrypted files from the University had been red herrings, designed to waste time and resources while keeping the real information hidden elsewhere. Could it be that the cottage fire had been set to destroy any of Dr Merton's records, leaving only the office "misdirection" files? If that were the case, then this was the first time that Barton and Brooks knew more than the murderer had predicted they would discover. The cottage arson was the murderer's first mistake; it was beginning to look like they were starting to take control of the case. If Dr Merton had been close to unravelling the truth, her discovery had come at a terrible personal cost.

The more Barton and Brooks uncovered, the more they realised that Dr Merton's death was not just a simple murder; it was carried out to protect a secret. Whoever was behind this was not only skilled in deception but also an extremely well-read historian.

As they prepared to take the next steps, Barton and Brooks set out to find the missing pieces of Dr Merton's research. They had leads to follow, including the mysterious "E" and the enigmatic "Source" mentioned in the journal. But they also knew they had to tread carefully: one wrong move, and they would never reveal the truth. The next step was to bring Chief Inspector Michael Dixon up to date with their findings and to discuss the possibility of a search warrant for Edward Voss's shop to find evidence of him being the mysterious "E."

Chapter 22

Whipton Barton walked through the echoing corridors of the Exeter Police Headquarters, the sound of his footsteps clicking on the institutional linoleum sounding like a metronome set to andante. It was late afternoon and he was seeing the Chief Inspector. Barton had arranged this meeting to show how the investigation had progressed in leaps and bounds since they last spoke, with new clues surfacing and a suspect emerging.

Barton paused outside Dixon's office door, straightening his tie and taking a deep breath before knocking.

"Come in," came Dixon's deep voice from within.

Barton pushed open the door and stepped inside. Dixon was sitting behind his desk, his eyes fixed on a report in front of him. He looked up as Barton entered, his expression giving nothing away. Barton had a brief flashback to being called to see the headmaster.

"Inspector Barton," Dixon greeted him with a smile. "Have a seat. I've gone over the interim report from your department," Dixon began, folding his hands on the desk. "It seems you've made some significant progress since we last spoke. What are your thoughts?"

Barton nodded, grateful for the opportunity to dive straight into the details. "Yes, sir. We have certainly moved forward, though each time we have found evidence, the case has grown more complicated. After our initial conversation,

I spoke with Professor Lowman, and he had some intriguing insights into Dr Merton's research."

Dixon raised an eyebrow, encouraging Barton to continue.

"According to Professor Lowman, the manuscript Dr Merton was piecing together is called the *Vita Regis,* and she believed that the fragments she had identified could have significant implications for our understanding of that era. He does have grave doubts about their authenticity, but he said that if Dr Merton's work were proven to be true, that would be enough to attract unwarranted attention."

Dixon leaned back in his chair, his gaze thoughtful. "Unwarranted attention from whom, exactly?"

"That he couldn't tell; he said he had very little to go on, and while Dr Merton had been in touch, she had shared very little," Barton admitted. "But there's more. Edward Voss's name has continued to come up during our investigation."

"Voss, you say?" Dixon mused, tapping a finger on the desk. "And how does he fit into all of this?"

"That's the question," Barton replied. "As you know, he left Dr Merton's employ around ten years ago. Well, since then, he has participated in other academic projects and now has his antiquarian bookshop near the Cathedral. However, he's made some remarks that suggest he may know more about her research than he's told us, and I think there's a definite feeling of resentment there. We've also found evidence that someone with advanced technical skills may have been helping Dr Merton encrypt her office files.

Dixon's eyes narrowed slightly. "So, you believe Voss may have been involved in securing Dr Merton's work, or in making sure it couldn't be accessed after her death?"

"We are not sure which, but it's a possibility we can't ignore."

Dixon sat in silence for a moment, processing the information. "So do you think Voss is the key to unlocking this mystery?"

"He certainly could be," Barton replied carefully.

"Currently, we're considering him a person of interest rather than a suspect. I'd like to interview him first without making any formal accusations. There's a lot we don't know about his relationship with Dr Merton, and I believe that speaking to him might shed some light on what happened."

Dixon nodded slowly, his expression serious. "You're right to be cautious. Voss could be a valuable source of information, but if he's involved, he'll be on guard – you'll need to approach this delicately."

"That's my intention, sir," Barton said. "However, I also believe that we should search Voss's shop. If he's been hiding anything, documents, correspondence, or even digital files, we'll likely find them there. I'd like to request a search warrant to ensure that we don't miss any crucial evidence."

Dixon leaned forward, his gaze sharp. "To be absolutely clear, you want a search warrant based on his potential involvement in Dr Merton's death, correct?"

"Yes," Barton confirmed. "Given the circumstances, I believe it's a justified course of action. We know Voss had a connection to Dr Merton, and we know her research was sensitive enough to attract attention. If Voss is hiding something, we need to find it before he has a chance to cover his tracks."

Dixon was silent for a long moment, then sighed. "A search warrant is a serious step, Barton. We need to be absolutely certain that we have probable cause. What else have you found that could support this?"

Barton took a deep breath, ready to present the final piece of the puzzle. "There's also the matter of Dr Merton's death. The initial autopsy and toxicology reports indicate that she was poisoned. However, the exact circumstances of her death are still unclear. We're looking into the possibility that she was killed in the Chapter House, but we haven't worked out if the murderer was there with her, how they could have got in and out, or how the poison was administered."

Dixon's eyes widened slightly. "Poison? That changes things. If Voss had access to her during her final days, or if he was involved in her research, he could have had the means and the opportunity to carry out such a poisoning."

"That's what we're trying to determine," Barton said. "There are still so many unanswered questions, but the pieces seem to be starting to come together. If Voss was involved in Dr Merton's death, then searching his shop could give us the evidence we need to connect him to the crime."

Dixon nodded. "You've certainly given me a lot to think about, Barton. I'll need to review the details carefully and speak to the CPS before making a decision about the search warrant. In the meantime, I suggest you proceed with the interview as planned. See what Voss has to say and be prepared for anything."

"I will," Barton assured him. "But there's one more thing I'd like to discuss."

Dixon raised an eyebrow, signalling for Barton to continue.

"During my initial investigation," Barton began, choosing his words carefully, "I've noticed that there's a certain... reluctance among some of the people involved to speak openly about Dr Merton's work. It's almost as if they're afraid of something, or someone. I remember what you said about Leonard Berger when we last spoke."

Dixon asked. "Are you suggesting that someone powerful might be involved in Dr Merton's death?"

"It's only a hunch, and I have no evidence to support it yet, but yes," Barton said.

Dixon was silent for a moment, his gaze distant as he considered Barton's words. "I've been in the police service long enough to know that there are cases where there are sometimes forces at play, forces that don't always operate within the boundaries of the law. If you're right, then this case could be one of them."

"That's why I'm asking for your advice," Barton said. "I need to know how to navigate these waters without putting the investigation, or myself, at risk."

Dixon sighed, leaning back in his chair. "You're in a delicate position, Barton, that's for sure. If there are powerful people involved, they'll be watching you closely."

Barton nodded, absorbing the advice. "Understood. Do you think it's possible that Voss could be connected to these people?"

"It's possible," Dixon admitted. "By all accounts, Voss is intelligent, and he's well-connected, so he could be acting on behalf of someone else, or he could be working alone. You'll need to find out which."

"I'll interview Voss as planned," Barton said. "And if I find anything that points to a larger conspiracy, I'll bring it to your attention immediately."

Dixon nodded, his expression softening slightly. "You're doing good work, Barton. Keep it up, and we will get to the bottom of this."

With that, the meeting drew to a close. Barton stood up, shaking Dixon's hand before turning to leave. As he walked back through the corridors of the headquarters, his mind was already planning his next move.

The interview with Edward Voss could be a turning point in the investigation, Barton knew that much. He felt Voss was the key to unravelling the mysteries surrounding Dr Merton's death. If he had been the one planning all this, being interviewed would also have been expected, and he would have been ready to protect himself if he felt threatened.

As Barton left the building and stepped into the cool autumnal Devon air, he took a deep breath.

The name Edward Voss was at the forefront of his thoughts as he walked to his car, its significance growing with every step. Voss was the strongest lead so far, but he knew he had to handle him carefully and extract the truth without awakening suspicions.

As he drove back to the station, Barton was already planning the interview with Voss, structuring the questions on how best to approach the enigmatic bookseller. He was determined to get the answers he needed, but he knew that Voss wouldn't make it easy. He was aware that one wrong move could undermine the entire investigation.

As Barton pulled into the station car park, he couldn't shake the feeling that the investigation was even closer to a breakthrough. Barton knew that the next few days would be critical. The interview with Voss, the search warrant for the shop, and the connections to Devon's elite all of these elements seemed to be converging into a single point.

Chapter 23

DI Barton phoned Edward Voss at his shop the following morning. He asked him if he could help clarify some things about Dr Merton and her research to help understand more about her work. Voss seemed very wary at first, but as Barton massaged his ego about how he was in a unique position and given his knowledge and experience, he may be of great help to the police in their enquiries, the more he warmed to the idea.

Barton had conducted countless interviews over the years. He knew how to read people, how to coax information out of them, and how to spot the subtle shifts in body language that gave away a lie, or guilt. As he prepared to interview Edward Voss, he couldn't shake the feeling that this one was going to be different. He knew from Lydia's description that Voss was an enigmatic man who had once been deeply embedded in the academic world, a world in which reputation was all, and everyone believed their research was the most important. His retreat into the quiet, insular life of an antiquarian bookseller and, in his spare time, a county set husband seemed an unusual move. Barton knew that Voss had worked with Dr Merton some years ago, but had he been in touch with her since ceasing to be her assistant?

When Barton entered the interview room, he found Voss already seated at the small table in the centre of the room. The man was calm, eerily so, his hands folded neatly in front of him, his body positioned still as a statue. His appearance was immaculate, his greying hair carefully combed, his clothing conservative and well-tailored. But it was his eyes that caught Barton's attention, cold, watchful and calculating.

"Mr Voss," Barton began as he took his seat across from him, "thank you for coming in to speak with me today."

Voss offered a thin, polite smile. "Of course, Inspector. I understand you have questions about Dr Merton. I will do my best to help."

Barton nodded, studying Voss's face. "Let's start with your relationship with Dr Merton. How well did you know her?"

Voss leaned back slightly in his chair, as if considering how much to reveal. "Evelyn and I first met just over twelve years ago when I was starting to work in academia after completing my MA. I was her research assistant for a time, one of many, I'm sure. We worked closely together on a number of projects, though our aims and ambitions eventually diverged."

Barton made a note of this. "What kind of projects were you working on?"

Voss shrugged, the movement elegant and dismissive. "Historical research, primarily. Evelyn was interested in medieval manuscripts, particularly those that had been overlooked or dismissed by other scholars. She had a knack for finding obscure texts and bringing them back into the light. My role was to assist with the translations, cataloguing and cross-referencing the material. It was tedious work, but necessary." All this was expressed with an affected air of boredom.

"Was this when she was working on the *Vita Regis* manuscript?" Barton asked, watching Voss carefully.

Voss's expression didn't change, but there was a brief pause before he answered. "Yes, that was one of the things we worked on together. The *Vita Regis* is an intriguing document, a chronicle that purported to reveal the existence of a secret group of nobles who manipulated the monarchy from behind the scenes. Evelyn was convinced that it was genuine, although as it was fragmented and very hard to verify, there was considerable debate about its authenticity."

"And what did you think?" Barton pressed. "Did you believe it was real?"

Voss hesitated, then smiled faintly. "I've always been a sceptic, Inspector. I saw the *Vita Regis* as an interesting idea, certainly, but whether it was a real document or a fake, well, that was for others to decide. My job was to help Evelyn present her evidence, not to make judgments about it."

Barton leaned forward slightly, his eyes narrowing. "You said your paths eventually diverged. How did you come to leave your position as Dr Merton's assistant?"

For the first time, Voss's calm air seemed to falter. He shifted in his seat, his fingers tightening slightly around the arms of his chair. "Academic life wasn't for me," he said, his voice carefully controlled. "I found the politics tiresome, the constant jockeying for position, funding and…the egos. I decided I would be happier pursuing my own interests, so I left Exeter University and took a few other short-term posts before opening my shop. It was a suitable transition for me, and I've never looked back."

Barton noted the slight tension in Voss's voice, the way his words seemed carefully chosen. "But your departure from academia wasn't entirely amicable, was it? There were rumours that you and Dr Merton had a falling out."

Voss's eyes flashed briefly with something that may have been anger, but it was quickly suppressed. "Rumours, Inspector, are just that…rumours. Evelyn and I had our differences, certainly, but there was no 'falling out.' We simply chose to go our separate ways."

Barton let the statement hang in the air for a moment before changing tack. "Tell me about your marriage, Mr Voss. How did you meet your wife, Victoria?"

Voss's expression softened slightly, though there was still

a guardedness about him. "Victoria and I met shortly after I left the University. We met looking for a rare book in a shop in Totnes. We struck up a conversation, and…well, one thing led to another. We were married within a year. We were in love, what can I say?"

"And how is your relationship with her family?" Barton asked, carefully watching Voss's reaction.

Voss's mouth tightened into a thin line. "The Bergers are…" he paused for a long time, "a prominent family in Exeter, as I'm sure you're aware. They had certain expectations for Victoria, and I'm not sure I've ever lived up to any of them. She was rebelling against the family at the time, and I suppose she chose the inappropriate. But we manage."

"You *manage*," Barton repeated, stressing the word. "What do you mean by that?"

Voss's eyes flicked up to meet Barton's, and for a moment the two men locked gazes. "Let's just say that I'm not the son-in-law they would have chosen for their darling Victoria," Voss replied, his voice carefully measured. "But we have made our own life together, partially separated from the expectations of her family."

Barton considered this for a moment before pressing on. "How has life outside academia been for you?"

Voss leaned back in his chair, his gaze growing distant. "Running the bookshop is quiet, even peaceful. I enjoy the solitude, the chance to immerse myself in the past without the distractions of the modern world. But I'd be lying if I said I didn't miss the intellectual challenge of academia from time to time. Then again, I don't have to deal with all those awful people, academics or students."

"Have you kept in touch with anyone from your academic days?" Barton asked.

Voss shook his head. "Not really. Most of my old colleagues have moved on, and so have I. My focus now is on my shop, my books and my own research."

"Your own research?" Barton inquired, intrigued. "Are you still working on historical projects?"

Voss hesitated, then nodded slowly. "I dabble, yes. There are still mysteries from the past that interest me, though I don't have the same resources I once did. I enjoy these challenges; they keep my mind sharp. These are gifts more like completing a cryptic crossword puzzle compared to real research; they merely entertain me." He said with a calculating smile.

Barton made a mental note of this. "What do you know about Dr Merton's research in the time leading up to her death? Did she mention anything to you about what she was working on?"

Voss's expression became guarded once more. "We hadn't spoken since I left the University, Inspector. I suspect she was still involved with the *Vita Regis* manuscript, as she had not yet published anything about it. Beyond that, I'm afraid I don't have much to offer."

Barton leaned in, his voice dropping to a more intense tone. "Did you know that Dr Merton was receiving threats? That she was concerned for her safety?"

Voss's eyes widened slightly, but he quickly regained his composure. "No, I didn't know that. I'm…surprised to hear it, to be honest, Evelyn was always very focused on her work, very driven. But threats? That seems very unlikely." His voice was slowing to a languid drawl that was beginning to annoy Barton.

"Unlikely, perhaps," Barton agreed, "but not unheard of in the world of academic research, especially when the stakes are high. It seems that Evelyn's research was leading her into some dangerous territory."

Voss shifted in his seat, his gaze flicking briefly to the door before returning to Barton. "I wouldn't know about that, Inspector. As I said, I haven't been involved in her work for a decade or more."

Barton looked at Voss in silence for a moment, weighing his next words carefully. "There's something else, Mr Voss, something that has come up during our investigation. You were Dr Merton's research assistant before Miranda Jackson, but there was a ten-year gap between your departure and Ms Jackson's appointment. Can you explain that?"

Voss's expression tightened. "Miranda is, I suppose you could say, my successor. Although I knew of the ten-year gap, I have no idea why. I met up with Ms Jackson recently in a café and had an interesting conversation with her. She had a lot of questions; however, she still has a lot to learn, and I fear she just does not have the ability."

Barton was shaken by the revelation of his meeting with Miranda, but pushed on, not wanting to show his surprise to Voss.

"And did you leave your job with Dr Merton willingly, or were you asked to leave?" Barton pressed, his voice steady.

Voss's jaw clenched, and for a moment, he seemed to struggle with his response. "I left because it was time for me to move on," he said finally. "Evelyn and I had different visions for the work, and it was clear that I was no longer needed. It was a mutual decision."

"One final question, Mr Voss. Do you think the *Vita Regis* is as important as Dr Merton believed?"

Voss's lips curved into a faint, enigmatic smile. "Who can say, Inspector? History is full of secrets, some of which are better left buried. She started working on it about a year before I left my assistant job. But if Evelyn was correct…well, then the *Vita Regis* could be the most important document of our time."

Barton leaned back in his chair, his gaze never leaving Voss's face. "Thank you for your time, Mr Voss. I appreciate your cooperation."

Voss nodded curtly, rising to his feet. "If there's anything else you need, Inspector, you know where to find me."

"Sure," said Barton. "There was one other thing. Did you ever help Dr Merton with encrypting her sensitive files? Our tech guys said there was a significant difference in the encrypted files from her office and the ones we managed to find at the cottage before it burnt down."

And there it was, Voss's shoulder tensed for the briefest moment. Barton was sure he had hit a nerve with that last question. There was a long silence before his measured reply came.

"For all her brilliance, Dr Merton didn't really do tech," said Voss, "and yes, I did some encrypted archiving for her. It has always been an interest of mine how something as simple as a digital record can be rendered impossible to open without sufficient knowledge, some sort of metaphor for research, I suppose."

As Voss left the room, Barton's mind was racing. There was something about Voss, something about the way he had answered, or hadn't answered, certain questions that left Barton uneasy: he was either hiding something, or perhaps even playing a game of cat and mouse with him. He always wanted to be one or two moves ahead, but the knowledge that they had obtained documents from the cottage appeared to have shaken him. Brooks was still busy going through these, and so Detective Sergeant Emily Tate had been observing the interview from behind the one-way glass. "What do you make of him, Emily?"

Tate frowned, crossing her arms "He's hiding something, that's for sure. He was too careful with his words, too guarded. And that bit about his own research, did you notice how vague he was? He didn't want to give us anything concrete."

Barton nodded in agreement. "Exactly. He's involved in this somehow, I can feel it. We need to dig deeper, find out what he's really been up to since he left academia."

Tate hesitated, then added, "There was one thing he said that struck me as odd. When he talked about the *Vita Regis,* he seemed almost…protective of it. Like he knows more about it than he's letting on."

Barton's eyes narrowed thoughtfully. "You're right. And there was something else: when I asked him about Evelyn's research, he was quick to deflect, to make it seem like he wasn't involved. But what if he was? What if he's been following her work all along?"

Tate raised an eyebrow. "You think he might have been trying to get his hands on the *Vita Regis* himself?"

"It's possible," Barton said slowly. "But there's more to it than that. He mentioned something about secrets better left buried. That's not the kind of thing you say as a researcher unless you're hiding something."

Tate nodded in agreement. "Then when you mentioned having documents from the cottage…"

"So, you saw that too," interrupted Barton.

"So, what's our next move, sir?" asked Emily.

Barton didn't hesitate. "We need to get a search warrant for Voss's shop. If he's been involved in anything shady, there's a good chance we'll find evidence there. If he has any connection to Evelyn's death, we need to uncover it before he has a chance to cover any more of his tracks. I think there is a chance he may be our arsonist as well."

Tate nodded, already pulling out her phone to make the necessary calls. "I'll check in with the Chief Inspector and get started on the paperwork."

As with everything else in this case, the interview with Voss had raised more questions than it had answered, but one thing was clear – Edward Voss was hiding something. A few hours later, Barton and Tate were standing outside Voss's bookshop. When Barton entered the shop, its overly bright bell announcing his arrival, Voss looked up, slightly startled. "Mr Voss, I have here a warrant to search your shop. We have reason to believe that you have documents here that will help us in our murder enquiry of the death of Dr Evelyn Merton."

Voss gasped and snatched the warrant from Barton's hand.

"Our officers will be here for a few hours, so I request that you close your shop for now. We will call you to come and lock up once we are finished," said Barton.

Voss gulped and nodded, picked up his jacket and left the shop without another word.

"Wow, he was really angry this time," said Emily.

"Start with the back room and his desk," Barton instructed Tate. "If he's hiding anything, it's likely to be there."

Tate nodded and headed towards the back of the shop, while Barton began to methodically search the front. He carefully examined each shelf, each drawer, looking for anything out of place.

It didn't take long for Tate to call out from the back room. "Inspector, I think I've found something."

Barton hurried to the back, where Tate was standing in front of a large filing cabinet, the keys still dangling in the lock. She had already opened the first drawer, revealing a collection of items that immediately caught Barton's attention.

Inside the cabinet were several old manuscripts, some of which appeared to be original medieval documents and what looked like a journal. But it was what lay beneath them that made Barton's heart skip a beat: an envelope, marked with Dr Evelyn Merton's name. Barton carefully opened the envelope, revealing a series of letters, letters that were filled with threats, warnings and ultimatums. They were addressed to Evelyn, arranged in a numbered sequence and ready to be sent, and they made it clear that Voss wanted her to stop her research into the *Vita Regis*. Also in the envelope was a USB drive, the identical make and capacity as the one they had found in Dr Merton's office.

"This is it," Barton said, his voice grim. "This is the evidence we needed. If Brooks could match the batch number and origin of this USB to the one we found in the office, then Voss is involved in this, no question about it. And if these letters are anything to go by, he's been trying to stop Evelyn from uncovering something dangerous, something he didn't want the world to know, or wanted to claim as his own."

Tate nodded, her expression serious. "We'll need to bring him in for questioning as a suspect, Inspector. This is more than enough to justify it."

Barton agreed. "Let's complete the search process in case there is more evidence, and then we'll find out exactly what he knows and then bring him in."

As he prepared to leave the shop, Barton couldn't help but feel a sense of foreboding. There was no turning back now; if Edward Voss was the key to unlocking the secrets of the *Vita Regis*, then Barton would have to make sure he didn't slip away.

Chapter 24

While the search of Voss's shop continued, Barton returned to his office and was looking out of the window of his office, the drizzle that had lasted all day making the view colourless. The day had been intense, filled with revelations, interviews and frustrating dead ends. Now, as he prepared for a crucial meeting with Miranda about her meeting with Voss, his thoughts were firmly on the next steps in the investigation. His unease grew as he thought about Miranda's involvement in the case. She had proven herself resourceful and fearless, but he couldn't shake the feeling that she could have crossed a line to discover a clue, one that could have put her and the investigation itself in serious danger. A knock at the door broke him out of his thoughts. Barton turned to see Miranda standing in the doorway, her expression tense. She had been preparing herself for this conversation.

"Come in, Miranda," Barton said, his voice steady but carrying an edge of concern. "We need to talk."

Miranda entered the office, closing the door behind her. She took a seat across from Barton, her hands clasped tightly in her lap. She was usually so composed, but today there was a nervousness about her that Barton hadn't previously seen.

Before he could say anything, Miranda blurted out, "I went to see Edward Voss!"

Barton's eyes narrowed, and he leaned forward, resting his elbows on the desk. "Now why would you do that?" His voice was calm. "Do you know the risk you've taken? More and more, I suspect Voss is not someone to be underestimated either physically or intellectually."

Miranda looked down at her hands, her voice steady but tinged with guilt. "I know it was dangerous and probably foolish, but I felt like I had to do it. I needed to understand what was going on, and I thought confronting him directly might give me some answers."

Barton sighed, leaning back in his chair. "Miranda, this isn't a game; this is my job. You've potentially put yourself in a lot of danger, and for what? What did you expect to find?"

Miranda looked up, meeting Barton's gaze full on. "I didn't know what to expect. But I did find something, something I think is important."

Barton's frustration turned to curiosity. If Miranda had uncovered something, despite his disapproval of her methods, he needed to know what it was.

Miranda hesitated for a moment before responding. "Voss was...unsettling. He's smart, very smart, and he knows it. But there's something off about him. He's arrogant, yes, but there's also a huge sense that he's carrying a huge grudge. I tried to ask him about Dr Merton's research, but he was evasive. He didn't give me any concrete answers, but he did drop a few hints."

"Hints? Like what?" said Barton

Miranda leaned forward slightly, lowering her voice as if sharing a secret. "He mentioned that Dr Merton was working on something big, something that could 'change everything.' He didn't elaborate, but he implied that he was both intrigued and bitter about it. Almost as if he felt he should have been part of it but was deliberately excluded, there was just something about him that made me doubt he was telling the truth."

Barton frowned. This could fit with what they already knew about Voss, his connection to Dr Merton, his departure from her mentorship, and his subsequent resentment. But it still didn't explain everything.

"Did he mention anything about the *Vita Regis* manuscript?" Barton asked.

Miranda shook her head. "No, but when I brought up her research, he did mention something about ancient texts and lost knowledge. It's possible he was referring to that, but he was careful not to say too much. It was almost like he was testing me, trying to see how much I knew."

Barton considered this. Voss was clearly playing a game, but what was his end goal? Was he just toying with them, or was there something more sinister at play?

"Did he say anything else that stood out?" Barton asked.

Miranda nodded. "There was one other thing. He mentioned that Dr Merton had become increasingly paranoid in the weeks leading up to her death. He said she was constantly looking over her shoulder, worried that someone was watching her. But he didn't say who. And to my knowledge, they hadn't met up since he left the University, so how would he know?"

Barton leaned back in his chair, processing everything Miranda had told him. "Miranda, I appreciate that you're trying to help, but you need to understand how dangerous this is. If Voss is our man, then he is not someone to be trifled with, and if he suspects that we're onto him, he could become dangerous. It may also be that your actions could jeopardise the investigation, allowing the murderer to get away with their crime through a legal technicality."

Miranda looked down, clearly troubled by Barton's words. "I didn't mean to cause any harm. I just wanted to help."

"I know," Barton said, his tone softening. "But you need to let us handle this from here. We're going to get to the bottom of this, but we have to do it the correct way. It isn't as exciting as the investigations shown on TV."

Miranda nodded, but Barton could tell that she was still on

edge. Barton knew that they were at a critical juncture in the investigation. The information Miranda had gathered from her meeting with Voss was valuable, but it wasn't enough. They needed more concrete evidence, something that could tie Voss directly to Dr Merton's research and - ultimately - to her death.

Miranda looked up, her eyes widening slightly. "Do you think he's involved in Dr Merton's death?"

"I don't know for sure," Barton admitted. "But he's definitely connected to her research, and that's reason enough to dig deeper. If he's involved, we'll find out."

Miranda nodded, her expression serious. "What do you want me to do?"

Barton hesitated for a moment. "For now, I need you to stay out of it. You've done more than enough, and I don't want you putting yourself at any further risk. Let us handle the investigation from here."

Miranda seemed to understand, though Barton could see the reluctance in her eyes. She had been a valuable ally during the investigation, but he knew that involving her any further could be dangerous for her.

"I'll keep you informed," Barton said. "But promise me you won't go off on your own again. If you hear or see anything suspicious, you come straight to me."

Miranda nodded and barely audibly said, "I promise."

"Before you go, can you tell me about Dr Merton's technical abilities. What do you know about her skills with technology, particularly encryption?"

Miranda nodded, glad to be on more solid ground. "Dr Merton was competent with technology, but she wasn't a specialist. She could handle the basics – emails, word processing, things like that – but when it came to more advanced tasks, she would have needed help. She was aware of her limitations and wasn't too proud to ask for assistance when necessary."

Barton took in this information, considering its implications. "So, it's unlikely that she could have carried out the sophisticated encryption of the files we found at her office by herself?"

"Yes," Miranda agreed. "I'd say it's certain someone else would have had to help her with that." Barton nodded. This aligned with what Saxon Brooks had discovered during his decryption efforts. The files from the University had been highly encrypted, far more so than the ones found at Dr Merton's cottage.

"We know it wasn't you who encrypted them, as the date stamp shows they were done before you became her assistant, according to Sergeant Brooks," said Barton.

"Do you have any idea who might have helped her?" Barton asked.

Miranda shook her head. "I don't know for sure, but it could have been one of her colleagues or someone else at the university IT team. There were very few people she trusted with things like that, but she never mentioned anyone specific to me."

The conversation with Miranda had given him valuable insights, but it had also confirmed his worst suspicions. The search of Voss's shop could be a critical turning point in the investigation; for now, he had to wait for the team to complete the search and process their findings.

Chapter 25

Edward Voss slammed the front door of his house, rattling the panes of glass, the sound echoing through the quiet suburban street. His chest heaved with the residual anger and frustration that had been simmering since the police had shown up at his shop with a search warrant. The audacity of it! He could barely comprehend what was happening to his shop, his private world, his sanctuary, invaded by strangers in uniforms, rifling through his belongings as if he were some common criminal. He marched through the dimly lit hallway, his mind racing, desperately trying to imagine what they may have found, how they might twist the truth to suit their narrative. Sure, he had secrets, who didn't? But he was no *common* criminal. Yet, here he was, under suspicion, his life unravelling before his eyes.

As he entered the living room, the first thing that greeted him was Victoria, his beautiful wife, lounging on the sofa with a glass of wine in her hand. She looked up at him from her book with an expression that was somewhere between boredom and disdain. She didn't ask where he had been or why he was home so early, nor did she express any concern about his obvious distress. Instead, she simply raised an eyebrow, a smirk playing at the corners of her mouth.

"Well, look who's finally home," she drawled, her voice dripping with sarcasm. "Did the little antiquarian have a rough day at the shop?"

Edward's temper flared instantly. The stress of the day, the violation of his privacy, the fear that was gnawing at him, all exploded in that moment. He had barely contained his anger all the way home.

"Do you have any idea what I've been through today?" he spat indignantly, his hands clenched into fists at his sides. "I have been interviewed by the police and right now they are searching my shop…our shop…probably tearing it apart as if I were some kind of criminal!"

Victoria took a slow sip of her wine, her eyes never leaving his. "And why do you think that is, Edward? You must have done something to attract their attention."

Her words were like pouring petrol onto a fire. Edward could feel the heat rising in his face, the pounding of his heart in his chest. He took a step closer to her, his voice low and dangerous. "I've done nothing wrong, and you know it. This is all because of that damned investigation into Evelyn's death. They're looking for someone to blame, and I'm the easiest target."

Victoria snorted, setting her glass down on the coffee table with a clink. "Evelyn, Evelyn, Evelyn. Is that all you can think about? Even now, after all this time, she's still controlling your life. You're pathetic, Edward."

The mention of Evelyn's name in that taunting tone felt like a knife twisting in Edward's gut. The relationship he'd had with Evelyn was complicated, tangled in a professional respect, an intellectual challenge, and something else he had never fully understood. Whatever it had been, he had tried to put it in the past. Now, with the investigation into her death, it had all come roaring back into his life, dredging up old wounds that had never fully healed.

"You don't know anything about what happened between me and Evelyn," Edward snapped. "So don't pretend you do."

"Oh, don't I?" Victoria shot back, her voice rising. "I know you were obsessed with her! I know you couldn't stop talking about her work, her brilliance, her 'potential.' You acted like she was the only thing that mattered in the world, while I, your wife, was nothing more than an afterthought!" She paused, "You even used to talk about her in your sleep," she spat the words with utter contempt.

"Don't twist this around," Edward warned, his voice shaking. "You're the one who's never supported me. You've always looked down on my work, belittled my efforts."

Victoria stood up, her own anger flaring. "Because it's all such a farce, so small time, Edward! You're not a businessman, you're not even a competent shopkeeper. Your so-called 'business' is a joke. You spend all your time chasing after dead men's papers and dusty old books, while our life, our real life, falls apart around you!"

Edward could feel his anger building, an invisible force pushing them towards an inevitable confrontation. He had never seen Victoria like this, so full of venom and spite, and it scared him. But it also further fuelled his anger, his sense of betrayal.

"After we married, you never gave a damn about what I was trying to accomplish. Was that because you had accomplished what you wanted at that point, your rebellion against your own family? You think you're so much better than me, don't you?" he shouted, taking another step closer to her. "You think you can just sit here, drinking your wine, while I try to keep us afloat? You think I'm useless, don't you?"

Victoria's eyes flashed with something dark and dangerous. "I don't think it, Edward. I know it. You've never been anything but a disappointment, a failed academic, a failed businessman and now a failed husband."

That was it. Something inside Edward snapped. All the years of frustration, of feeling like he wasn't good enough, of watching his dreams slip away, it all came pouring out in a blind rage. He lunged at Victoria, his hands reaching for her as if he could silence her cruel words by sheer force.

Victoria, caught off guard, stumbled back, but she wasn't afraid. If anything, her anger matched his, meeting fire with fire. She pushed him back with both hands, her face twisted in fury.

"Don't you dare touch me!" she screamed. "You're nothing, Edward! Nothing!"

But Edward wasn't listening. His world had narrowed to a single point, his vision blurred with rage. He reached for her again, and this time his hand connected with her face, his ring cutting into her cheek.

Victoria gasped, more from shock than pain, her hand flying to the spot where he had struck her. Blood welled up beneath her fingers, the bright red a stark contrast against her pale skin. She stared at him, her eyes wide with disbelief.

For a moment, time seemed to stop. Edward, too, was frozen, his hand still outstretched, his mind struggling to process what he had just done. The room was deathly silent, the only sound the rapid, uneven breaths from both husband and wife, and the steady tick of the grandfather clock.

Then, Victoria's shock gave way to something else, something hurtful, more calculating. Her lips curled into a cruel smile, even as blood trickled down her cheek.

"You've really done it now, Edward," she said, her voice cold as ice. "You think you're the one with the power here? You think you can just hit me and get away with it?"

Edward's heart pounded in his chest, fear and regret crashing over him in waves. What had he just done to the woman he once loved enough to marry? "Victoria, I didn't mean..."

"Shut up!" she snapped, cutting him off. "I don't want to hear your pathetic excuses. My father is going to hear about this. He's going to hear everything, and when he does, you're going to wish you'd never even met me."

Panic set in, gripping Edward's heart in a vice. He knew

she wasn't bluffing. He was frightened of Victoria's father; he was a powerful man, with connections that reached far beyond their quiet little city. If he got involved, Edward's life – his already precarious, fragile life – would be destroyed.

"Victoria, please," he pleaded, desperation creeping into his voice. "We can talk about this. I'm sorry, I didn't mean to…"

But Victoria wasn't listening. She stepped back, her eyes blazing with fury and triumph. "Get out, Edward. Get out of this house. Get out of my house and don't you dare come back."

Edward stood there, rooted to the spot, his mind racing. Part of him wanted to fight, to refuse to be driven out of his own home. But another part, the part that had been battered and bruised by years of failure and disappointment, knew he had no choice. Victoria had won, and there was nothing he could do to change that.

Slowly, Edward turned away, his shoulders slumping in defeat. He started towards the door, his mind numb, his body moving on autopilot. As he passed the shelf lined with Victoria's prized collection of delicate porcelain ornaments, in a fit of rage, he swept his arm across the shelf, sending the ornaments crashing to the floor. The sound of breaking porcelain filled the room, sharp and jarring, echoing the destruction of their marriage, of everything they had once shared. Victoria didn't flinch. She just watched him with cold, detached eyes, as if he were nothing more than a stranger, nothing more than an unpleasant memory to be discarded.

Without another word, Edward stormed out of the house, slamming the door behind him, once again rattling the windows. Outside, the afternoon was shifting to the cool and stillness of evening, a stark contrast to the turmoil raging inside him. He stood on the front step for a moment, breathing hard, trying to make sense of what had just happened.

But there was no sense to be found. Only the cold, hard reality that he had lost everything: his wife, his home, his dignity. And all because of Evelyn Merton, the woman who had haunted his thoughts for years, and still now, even in death.

As he walked away from the house, Edward's mind whirled with thoughts of revenge, of reclaiming what was his, of proving to everyone – Victoria, her father, the police – that he was a force to be reckoned with. At that moment, his phone rang. It was one of the constables at his shop who asked him to return to lock up for the night. He tried to steady his voice as he spoke to the officer and then headed back to the shop. I guess I'll be sleeping there tonight anyway, he thought to himself.

Chapter 26

Victoria Berger sat in the back seat of the chauffeur-driven black Mercedes, her hand delicately resting on the small cut on her cheek, the wound still fresh and the bruise throbbing from the previous night's confrontation with Edward. The early morning sun filtered through the tinted windows, casting a muted light on her face, which was impeccably made-up and composed. Victoria's father, a man of significant influence and power, had wasted no time ensuring she had the best legal representation by using the Berger family solicitor. Jackson Ferris sat beside her, his expression as unreadable as ever; he was wearing an immaculately tailored suit, silk shirt and tie, and he smelt expensive. As the car pulled up to the police station, Victoria took a deep breath. She wasn't particularly nervous; Victoria was a woman who knew how to handle herself in difficult situations, and as a rule, nerves were not something she would let get in her way. Reporting her husband's assault was going to change the course of both their lives. After last night's violent outburst, she knew it was a step that had to be taken, and in many ways it was a relief, perhaps even the dawning of a new chapter in her life.

The moment the car stopped, Ferris came round to open her door. Victoria stepped out, her movements poised, every inch the picture of a woman in control; understated but undeniably classy, she had dressed to be respected. Together, they walked up the stone steps and into the station, where the clinical smell of industrial disinfectant and the low hum of voices greeted them.

At the front desk, a tired-looking officer glanced up, his eyes widening as he took in the pair in front of him. It wasn't every day that someone like Victoria Berger walked into a police station accompanied by a well-known solicitor. The officer straightened up, immediately attempting a more professional appearance, which he didn't really pull off.

"Good morning, ma'am, sir," he said, his tone polite. "How can I assist you today?"

"I'm here to report an assault," Victoria said, her voice steady and calm, though there was a steeliness that made the officer pay attention. "By my husband, Edward Voss."

The officer blinked, taken aback by the directness of her statement. "Of course, ma'am. If you'll follow me, I'll take you to someone who can help."

Victoria and Ferris were led through a series of corridors to one of the nondescript interview rooms. It was a far cry from the luxurious surroundings Victoria was used to, but she barely registered her surroundings. She was focused on the task at hand, to protect herself and ensure that Edward was held accountable for his actions.

After a few moments, the door opened, and Barton entered the room. He took a seat across from her. "Mrs Berger", Barton began, his voice deep and measured. "I'm Detective Inspector Whipton Barton. I understand you're here to report an assault. Are you happy to be interviewed without a woman officer present?"

"That's Ms Berger, and yes, that's correct," Victoria replied, her tone precise. She turned slightly, gesturing to Ferris. "I have my solicitor, Jackson Ferris, who'll be present for the interview with me, so no one else needs to be here."

Barton nodded in acknowledgement, his gaze shifting briefly to Ferris before returning to Victoria. "Very well. I need you to tell me exactly what happened. Can you start by telling me, in your own words, what happened?"

Victoria took a deep breath, knowing that how she presented herself now would be crucial. "It began as an argument," she said, her voice clear. "Edward had come home in a state of extreme agitation. He was angry, angrier than I've ever seen him. His shop had just been subjected to a search by the police, and he was furious about it."

Barton nodded, jotting down notes as she spoke. "And what was the argument about?"

"It was about many things," Victoria replied, choosing her words carefully. "His business, his frustrations, but it quickly escalated. He's been under a lot of stress lately, ever since the death of Dr Evelyn Merton. He's been acting strangely. Last night, it all came to a head. He…he struck me during the argument."

She gently touched the cut on her cheek, making sure Barton could see the evidence of the assault. "I didn't provoke him," she added quickly. "If anything, I was trying to calm him down, but he wasn't in a state to listen. He was consumed by anger."

Ferris, who had been silent until now, leaned forward. "Detective Inspector, it's important to note that my client is not seeking retribution. Her main concern is her own safety and ensuring that her husband receives the help he clearly needs. However, given the circumstances, she felt it necessary to involve the authorities."

Barton looked from Ferris to Victoria, his expression thoughtful. "I appreciate your position, Ms Berger, but I need to ask some more specific questions about your husband's behaviour leading up to the incident. You mentioned that he's been acting strangely since Dr Merton's death. Can you elaborate on that?"

Victoria hesitated for a moment, her mind racing as she tried to decide how much to reveal. "Edward has always been…intense, especially when it comes to his work. In recent years, when Dr Merton's name was mentioned, he would become introspective. Then he started withdrawing from me, spending more time at the shop, staying out late. He wouldn't tell me what he was working on, but I could tell it was something important to him, something related to Dr Merton."

Barton's pen paused over his notebook. "Do you know what that might have been?"

"No," Victoria said, shaking her head. "He was very secretive about it. But whatever it was, it was consuming him. He wasn't sleeping properly, and when he was home, then since her death, he has always been on edge, as if he was expecting something to happen."

Barton leaned back in his chair, studying Victoria closely. "Ms Berger, where was your husband on the night Dr Merton was murdered?"

Victoria's eyes widened slightly at the directness of the question, but she recovered quickly. "I…I don't know. He wasn't home, that's for certain. He told me he was working late at the shop, but I can't confirm that. We…we've been living somewhat separate lives lately."

Barton nodded slowly, his gaze never leaving her face. "So, you can't provide an alibi for him?"

"No, I can't," Victoria admitted, her voice tinged with frustration. "But that doesn't mean he's guilty of anything. Edward is many things, but a murderer. I can't believe that."

"But you're here to report him for assault," Barton pointed out.

Victoria sighed, her composure faltering for the first time. "Because I'm scared, Chief Inspector, Edward isn't the man I married. He's changed, and I don't know what he's capable of anymore. I'm not saying he killed Dr Merton, but… something's wrong. He's hiding something, and I'm afraid of what that might be."

Barton's gaze softened slightly as he absorbed her words. He could see that Victoria was in a difficult position, torn between loyalty to her family and fear for her safety. But he also knew that her testimony could be crucial in the investigation.

"Ms Berger," he said after a moment, "based on what you've told us, we can certainly bring Mr Voss in for questioning about the assault. This will give us the opportunity to hold him for a short while while we investigate further. However, I need you to understand that this could lead to other charges if we find evidence linking him to Dr Merton's death."

"I understand," Victoria said quietly. "I'm not trying to protect him, Detective Inspector. I just want the truth to come out, whatever that truth may be."

Ferris leaned forward again, his expression carefully neutral. "My client has been fully cooperative, Detective Inspector. I trust that will be taken into account during your investigation."

"Of course," Barton replied, his tone professional. "Thank you for your cooperation, Ms Berger. We'll keep you informed of any developments – should I contact you or Mr Ferris?" Ferris said calmly, "Probably both of us would be best. I will also be keeping Mr Berger informed as well."

As Victoria and Ferris walked back to the car, Ferris spoke up, his voice low and measured. "You did the right thing, Victoria. This was the only way to protect yourself."

"What if…what if Edward had nothing to do with Dr Merton's death? Murmured Victoria quietly to herself.

Ferris stopped and turned to face her, his expression serious. "If he's innocent, the investigation will prove that. But if he's not, then you've saved yourself from living in a potentially dangerous situation. Either way, this was necessary. I suggest you move in with your father for a few days while the investigation continues. I assume Edward doesn't have keys to that house, at least?"

Victoria nodded, though her heart was heavy. She knew Ferris was right; this was necessary, but it didn't make the guilt any less real. She had once loved Edward, had shared a life with him, and now she was the one who might be bringing that life crashing down around him.

When they reached the car, Victoria glanced back at the police station, a sense of finality settling over her. There was no turning back now. The wheels had been set in motion, and whatever happened next was out of her hands.

Back in the station, Barton sat in his office, reviewing his notes from the interview. On the surface, it seemed straightforward, an assault by a husband on his wife, driven by anger and frustration. But the more Barton thought about it, the more he saw that this was yet more evidence of Voss's volatility.

Edward Voss was already a person of interest in Dr Merton's murder investigation. The search of his shop had yielded some intriguing leads connecting him to Dr Merton, but nothing as yet to connect him directly to her murder. Now, with the assault charge hanging over him, Barton had the opportunity to bring Voss in for questioning a second time and buy them a little time to dig deeper into his connection to Dr Merton.

There was something else that bothered Barton, the way Victoria had described her husband's recent behaviour. It wasn't just the assault that concerned him; it was the suggestion that Voss had been hiding something, that he had been consumed by some dark obsession. Barton knew that such behaviour could be indicative of a guilty conscience, or it could be the result of something else entirely.

Sergeant Emma Phillips, on Barton's team, interrupted his thoughts with a knock on the door. "Sir, I've got the preliminary report on the search of Voss's shop," she said, handing him a folder. "Nothing conclusive as yet, but there are some items that might warrant further investigation."

Barton opened the folder and quickly scanned the contents. There were references in the recovered journal to some old manuscripts, a collection of correspondence, and a few financial records that looked out of place. Nothing that screamed 'guilty,' but enough to raise an eyebrow.

"Good work, Phillips. Oh yes, has Saxon been given the USB stick from the shop to compare with the one from Dr Merton's office?" Barton asked, setting the folder aside.

"He's on it now, sir," she replied.

"I want to bring Voss in for questioning as soon as possible. We'll start with the assault charge and see where it leads us."

Phillips nodded, her expression serious. "Understood, sir. Do you think he's our murderer?"

Barton leaned back in his chair. "I don't know for sure yet, Phillips. But there's something about this whole situation that doesn't sit right with me. Voss is hiding something, and we have to find out what it is."

As the day wore on, Barton continued to piece together the puzzle that was Edward Voss. On one hand, he was this man who ran a small antiquarian shop, a man who had once been a respected academic, a man who had a complicated relationship with Dr Merton, and on the other, a man who had assaulted his wife in a fit of rage. But which of these men was the real Edward Voss? And how did he fit into the larger picture of Dr Merton's murder?

Barton knew that when Voss was arrested and in custody, they could continue to investigate. It wasn't a perfect solution, but it was the best option they had at the moment.

He also knew that they needed to tread carefully. Voss was clearly a man under immense pressure, and pushing him too hard could cause him to either shut down completely or lash out even more violently. Barton needed to uncover the truth without driving him into a corner.

As he continued to review the evidence, Barton's thoughts kept returning to Victoria Berger's words: "He's hiding something, and I'm afraid of what that might be."

By the time Barton was ready to call it a day, he had a clear plan in mind. The first step was to arrest Edward Voss on the assault charge, which would give them the opportunity they needed for the second interview. Barton knew that the real challenge was to get Voss to open up about his relationship with Dr Merton and what he had been doing in the days leading up to her murder.

Edward Voss had returned to Victoria's house that evening to collect some things and had been taken aback that she wasn't there. There was just a note on the shelf where the porcelain collection had been, saying, "Gone to Dad's, don't follow me if you know what's good for you." He stayed in the house that night, and he was arrested the following day.

The air was heavy with the promise of heavier rain, and the street was empty. Both the shop and the house had been watched overnight and that morning, so Barton knew precisely where Voss was as he led the team up the path to Voss's home at the top of Pennsylvania Road, their footsteps muffled on the wet pavement. There was no sense of satisfaction in the arrest, no feeling of triumph. Just a feeling, they were about to take a significant step forward in the investigation.

Voss was arrested for the assault on Victoria Berger. The interview with Victoria had given them enough to arrest, charge and hold him in custody. When Barton and his officers knocked on Voss's door, they were met with a man who seemed to have been expecting them. Voss's eyes were tired and hollow, his face drawn with the fatigue of a man who had spent too long running from his own shadow. He had not gone to open his shop that day and offered no resistance, merely raising his hands in a gesture of surrender as they placed the handcuffs around his wrists. Barton watched him carefully, noting the tension in his shoulders, the way his eyes darted around as if searching for an escape. Voss looked like a man on the edge, this time neither in control nor prepared. Barton knew that he would need to proceed with caution.

When Barton got back to the station later that afternoon, Voss was already in the interview room "Mr Voss," Barton said, "We have a few questions we'd like to ask you about the events of the last few days."

Voss's eyes narrowed, his jaw clenched. "I don't want a resolution, and more importantly, I don't have anything to say to you."

Barton smiled slightly, taken aback by Voss's hostility. "That's your right, Mr Voss. But I do think it would be in your best interest to cooperate. After all, the sooner we get to the bottom of this, the sooner you can get back to your life."

Voss didn't respond, his silence speaking volumes. Barton could see the fear and anger simmering just below the surface, and he knew that it was only a matter of time before something gave way.

As the interview began, Barton's opening gambit was to keep his questions focused on the assault charge, knowing that it was the key to keeping Voss in custody while they continued to investigate. But as the conversation progressed, Barton carefully began to steer it towards Dr Merton, probing gently but persistently for any information that might shed light on Voss's connection to the murdered woman.

Voss remained tight-lipped, refusing to give anything away, but Barton wasn't discouraged. He could see the cracks starting to form, the pressure building as Voss struggled to maintain his composure. Barton knew that it was only a matter of time before those cracks widened, revealing the truth that Edward Voss had been so desperately trying to hide. It was clear Voss wasn't going to cooperate today, so Barton terminated the interview, and Voss was led away to the custody cells.

Just before he was about to go home, Saxon burst into his office with as much glee and energy as Barton had ever seen in him. "Bingo!" He shouted loud enough for the officers in the open office to look up in surprise.

"What is it?" Barton asked in surprise. "The USB from the shop – it's from the same batch as the one from the office, but more importantly, the files on it are encrypted in the same way. It's like a digital version of handwriting – all coders have a unique digital style when writing lines of code. This ties Voss to the coded files from Dr Merton's office."

Chapter 27

The sun had long since set, casting the small town of Topsham into the embrace of a quiet, early autumnal night. Inside the Barton residence, the warm glow of the fire filled the living room with a comforting light. Barton sat in his favourite armchair, his brow furrowed as he stared at the stack of papers on the small table beside him. Lydia sat across from him on the sofa, a cup of chamomile tea cradled in her hands. At their feet, Pip stretched out full-length, snoring softly, his sides rising and falling in a peaceful rhythm, giving the whole room a homely, soporific air.

Lydia studied her husband's face, picking up on the telltale signs of frustration etched into his features. She had seen that look many times before, usually when he was wrestling with a particularly challenging case. This time, she knew, was different; the murder of Dr Evelyn Merton had cast a shadow over their lives, not just because of its complexity but because Evelyn had been her friend.

"What's on your mind, Whip?" Lydia asked gently, setting her tea down on the table beside her. "You've been staring at those papers for the best part of an hour."

Whipton glanced up at his wife, giving her a slight smile. Lydia had always been able to read him like a book. It was one of the many things he loved about her, their deep understanding of one another, the way she could offer insight when he was stuck.

"It's this case, Lyd," he said, running a hand through his greying hair. "It's like trying to piece together a puzzle where half the pieces are missing. Every time I think I'm getting somewhere, something else crops up that throws everything into question."

Lydia nodded, her expression thoughtful. "The *Vita Regis*, you mean?"

Whipton sighed and leaned back in his chair, his eyes drifting to the fireplace. The *Vita Regis*, a mysterious, fragmented manuscript that had somehow become entangled in the investigation, had been a thorn in his side from the beginning. Evelyn had been researching it before her death, but the more Whipton dug into it, the less it seemed to make sense. And now, with Edward Voss, a man with a penchant for secrecy and manipulation, coming into the picture, the whole thing had become even more complex.

"Among other things," Whipton replied, his voice heavy with frustration. "The *Vita Regis* is part of it, sure. But it's not just that. It's everything: Voss's involvement, Evelyn's secretive way of working, the way the whole thing feels like it's been designed to confuse us. I can't shake the feeling that I'm missing something really obvious."

Lydia sipped her tea, thinking as she processed what her husband had said. She had followed the case closely, not just because of her connection to Evelyn but because it had captured her curiosity. The *Vita Regis* had seemed like the key to understanding Evelyn's murder at first, but as the investigation had progressed, Lydia had started to doubt it was as important as everyone believed.

"I am beginning to think," Barton began slowly, his eyes narrowing in thought, "what if the *Vita Regis* isn't real?"

Lydia's gaze snapped back to him, a frown creasing his brow. She had done some digging of her own; while there was a lot of information about the Edward Confessor document, there seemed to be nothing concrete about the *Vita Regis*.

"What do you mean?" She asked.

"I mean, what if the *Vita Regis* isn't what it seems?" Barton clarified, setting his tea aside and leaning forward slightly. "What if it has no connection to Evelyn's murder at all, and instead, it's been made up or exaggerated to obfuscate the case?"

Whipton stared at her, the idea slowly making more sense now he had said it out loud. It was a bold suggestion, one that hadn't occurred to him until just now. The *Vita Regis* had been treated as a central piece of evidence, something that could explain why Evelyn was killed. What if it was nothing more than a red herring?

"Go on," Lydia said slowly, her interest piqued. This idea seemed to back up her research findings.

"Think about it," Barton continued, his voice gaining confidence as he fleshed out his theory. "Edward Voss is a man with a deep knowledge of antiquities, manuscripts and history. If anyone could fabricate a story about a lost manuscript and make it seem credible, it would be him. Combine that with the fact that Evelyn conducted her research in near-total secrecy, and it's not hard to imagine that no one would know if the *Vita Regis* was real."

Lydia nodded slowly, the pieces finally starting to fall into place. "So, you're saying that Voss might have created this story about the *Vita Regis* to throw you off the scent. To make it look like Evelyn's murder was connected to her research when, in fact, it was about something else entirely?"

Whipton felt a surge of excitement at the possibility. It made sense, more sense than the tangled web of theories and speculation they'd been chasing until now. If the *Vita Regis* was a fabrication, then it explained why the investigation had been so frustratingly complex, why every lead seemed to finish up in a dead end. Voss could have used his expertise to craft a story that would ensnare the police in a labyrinth of false clues and misdirection.

"But why would Voss do that?" Lydia asked, wanting to explore every angle. "Why go to all that trouble just to cover up a simple motive like jealousy or revenge?"

"Because he's clever and hell hath no fury like an academic scorned! Perhaps he was secretly in love with her, and she spurned him," Barton replied. "He was clever enough to know that a straightforward motive might eventually be uncovered. But if he could make the case seem more complicated, if he could create a narrative that pulled us in a completely different direction, then he'd have a much better chance of getting away with it. Voss has been involved in Evelyn's life in some capacity for a long time. He would have known about her secretive research habits from his time as her assistant, and he could have exploited that to his advantage."

Lydia sat in silence for a moment, absorbing what Whipton had said. It was a theory that fitted the facts in a way that nothing else had. If Voss had indeed fabricated the story of the *Vita Regis*, then it would explain the inconsistencies and the dead ends that had plagued the investigation; it also confirmed Professor Lowman's thought that it could indeed be a hoax and it would now give Whipton a whole new way to approach the case, one that focused on Voss's motives rather than the academic and historical distractions he had thrown in their path.

Pip shifted in his sleep, his soft snores breaking the silence in the room. Whipton glanced down at the dog, then back up at Lydia, a thoughtful expression on his face.

"I think you're onto something, Whip," she said finally. "If Voss is the one who's been manipulating the narrative, then you need to start looking at this case with fresh eyes. You can now strip away all the noise and distraction and focus on the core, on Voss's relationships, his behaviour and his motives."

Barton smiled, pleased that his idea had resonated with Lydia. "It's worth considering, at least sometimes, the simplest explanations are the ones we overlook because we're so caught up in the complexity."

Whipton was already thinking about how he could approach the investigation from this new angle. There were still many questions that needed answers: what exactly Voss's motive was, how he had managed to plant the story of the *Vita Regis*, and whether anyone else was involved, but this new theory gave him a renewed sense of purpose.

"I'll need to reexamine everything," Whipton said. "Look at the evidence with this theory in mind, see if there are any clues we missed because we were too focused on the *Vita Regis*. We'll need to interview Voss again, but this time, we'll approach it differently. We'll probe his personal life, his relationship with Evelyn, and see if we can get him to slip up."

Lydia nodded in agreement. "And don't forget to consider the possibility that others might be in on the deception as well. If Voss was capable of creating this elaborate distraction, he might have had help, someone who could corroborate the story or provide additional layers of deception."

Whipton's eyes narrowed as he considered this. "You're right. We can't rule out that possibility." Lydia leaned back against the sofa, relieved by Whipton's renewed energy about the case.

Whipton reached across the space between them, taking her hand in his. "I couldn't do any of it without you, Lyd. You always help me see things more clearly."

She squeezed his hand, a warm smile on her face. "That's what partners are for."

The next morning, Whipton Barton arrived at the station very early with a renewed sense of determination; he had also had his first good night's sleep since they had started investigating Evelyn Merton's death. He was eager to share this fresh perspective on the case with his team. As he walked through the familiar corridors of the police station, his mind was already working through the steps they needed to take.

In the briefing room, his team was gathered, was already waiting for his instructions. Barton wasted no time in laying out the new approach.

"I think we may have been looking at this case all wrong," he began. "Up until now, we've been treating the *Vita Regis* as the central piece of this investigation, as if Evelyn's murder was connected to her research. But what if it's not? What if the *Vita Regis* is irrelevant, designed to throw us off the real trail?"

The officers exchanged glances, clearly intrigued by this new line of thinking.

"I've been going over the evidence," Barton continued, "and there are too many inconsistencies, too many dead ends that don't add up. They always appear to lead back to Voss. He has the knowledge and the resources to create a convincing story about a lost manuscript; he could have used that story to distract us from his real motive, whatever that may be."

Detective Sergeant Emma Phillips raised her hand. "So, you think Voss killed Dr Merton for personal reasons, and he had made up the *Vita Regis* to humiliate her?"

"That's exactly what I'm suggesting," Barton replied. "We need to shift our focus away from the manuscript and start looking at Voss's personal life, his relationships, and his behaviour in the days leading up to the murder. We also need to consider the possibility that he had help, someone who could corroborate his story or provide additional layers of deception."

Phillips nodded thoughtfully. "It's a bold theory, sir, but it does make sense. We've been chasing after this manuscript as if it's the key to everything, but maybe we've been looking in the wrong place."

Barton could see his team had had their curiosity aroused by this new angle. "I want everyone to go back over every piece of evidence with fresh eyes," he instructed. "Look for anything that supports this theory, anything that suggests the *Vita Regis* was a fabrication or that Voss had a personal motive for killing Evelyn. And I need to interview Voss again, but this time, we'll be approaching it differently. We'll be looking for signs of deception, inconsistencies in his story, and anything that points to his true motive. I suspect he will not have anticipated that."

The case had taken a new direction, one that Barton felt for the first time more confident in pursuing.

By the end of the day, more connections had been made than had been made in the rest of the investigation. Saxon's tech connections to the evidence picked up from Voss's shop, added to these, his assault on Victoria Berger showed a man with dangerous anger issues. When Barton left for the night, he felt that, for the first time in ages, real progress had been made. They had had to release Voss from custody, bailed him on condition that he stay at his house. Officers had been stationed outside to ensure he complied.

Later that evening, after a long day at the station, Whipton returned home to find Lydia waiting for him with a warm meal and a welcoming smile. Pip was already curled up in his usual spot by the fireplace, and the house felt like a sanctuary after the intensity of the day.

"How did it go?" Lydia asked as they sat down to dinner.

"It went well," Whipton replied, a note of satisfaction in his voice. "The team is working on the new approach. We're going to start looking at the case from a different angle, focusing on Voss's motives rather than the *Vita Regis*."

They ate in comfortable silence for a few moments, the warmth of the fire and the peaceful atmosphere of their home wrapping around them like a comforting blanket. As they cleared the table and settled in for the evening, Pip snoring contentedly in his basket, Whipton felt a sense of peace he hadn't experienced since the case began.

Chapter 28

The next day was spent reassessing all the reports and evidence and seeing if they made any more sense set against the new simpler approach. If the *Vita Regis* was a hoax, then suddenly more of the pieces were beginning to make sense.

Brooks was still going through the files from the cottage USB and had also decrypted the USB drive that had been found in Voss's shop. Having broken the code on the office USB, this simply involved adopting the same process, and soon, much was revealed. It appeared that the finances of the shop were very shaky and there had been a lot of expenditure on medieval manuscripts going back to even before the shop had opened, although they had never appeared on the inventory. (A little creative accounting as well, thought Brooks). The interesting part was that these purchases were never sold to customers, nor did they appear in the shop's manuscript archive.

DS Emily Tate was looking through the personal folder found in the office and comparing this with the notebook found in the burnt tin after the fire, Dr Merton's journals (with particular focus on her feelings) and the letters found in Voss's shop. She also wanted to try and establish a link between E. and Edward Voss, other than the coincidence of the initials. Dr Merton had certainly been targeted in two ways. Firstly, personal attacks and threats dating back over at least ten years, Post-it notes with aggressive quotes and thoughts aimed at undermining her confidence. This could also account for her increasing paranoia around her work; the less self-assured she was, the easier it would be to contain the hoax until after publication. Secondly, the gradual reveal of how the *Vita Regis* hoax was built, stretching back well over ten years. Looking at it afresh from this new perspective, the whole story seemed outlandish. A council of powerful landowners running the country with a monarch purely as a front, it had the feel of a deep conspiracy theory that could be found in the darker corners of the Internet. Yet the drip feeding of clues had been done so subtly that it seemed to build to being a plausible story.

Meanwhile, DS Emma Phillips returned to the University HR department to dig deeper into Voss's dismissal. The whole issue had been dealt with internally, so his departure and any scandal would not make the press. However, the details finally emerged after Philips emphasised this was a key part of a murder enquiry and that took precedent over any potential public relations problems. She had been given confirmation about the notes being left and how Dr Merton felt she had to move off campus because they had been posted by hand to her flat. The University had kept her home address redacted from all but her confidential personnel file to try to keep her from being further bothered. The notes had never proven to be from Voss at the time, but now there seemed to be a strong circumstantial connection, strengthened by Dr Merton's feelings in her journals.

By the end of the day, when the team got together to share their findings, the case seemed much clearer than at any previous stage of the investigation. There appeared to be a possible motive; they knew she had been poisoned, and when she died, but even though they had a potential suspect, they couldn't yet connect him to the crime.

It was a cool evening, and the comforting familiarity of home beckoned to Barton as he walked through the front door. The day had been long, filled with new revelations and challenging discussions about the case. Not so long ago, he had been wrestling with theories and counter-theories, each one more complex than the last. Now there seemed to be an order emerging from the chaos, and that, for the first time, felt like progress. He knew he would also be interviewing Voss the next morning.

Stepping into the warm, inviting hallway, he hoped to find a brief reprieve from the whirlwind of the investigation. However, the moment he entered, he noticed something unusual. A murmur of soft voices drifted from the living room, carrying a tone of intense discussion. Curious, Barton moved quietly towards the sound, obviously recognising one voice as Lydia's, but the other took a moment to place. As he rounded the corner, the sight that met his eyes was unexpected but not unwelcome: Lydia and Miranda were seated on the sofa, engrossed in conversation.

The small table before them held several empty mugs, the remnants of a pot of tea, a plate of biscuits, and a few scattered papers. They were so deep in discussion that neither woman noticed Barton's arrival at first. He stood there for a moment, observing the scene with a quiet smile. It wasn't often that Lydia had a friend over, and seeing her so animated, so engaged, reminded him of the woman he'd fallen in love with.

Finally, Lydia looked up and spotted him. Her eyes widened in surprise, followed by a warm smile. "Whip! We didn't hear you come in."

Miranda turned in her seat, offering Barton a nod of greeting. "Detective Inspector, good evening."

"Good evening, Miranda," Barton replied, stepping fully into the room. "It's nice to see you here. Please let's drop the formality, as you are friends with Lydia. Whipton is fine – unless we are at the station," he said with a smile.

"I hope you don't mind me dropping by," Miranda said.

"Lydia and I got to talking about Evelyn's work, and, well, one thing led to another. I've been here a lot longer than I planned."

"Not at all," Barton assured her, waving away any concern. "I'm glad you're here. The two of you seem to be having a good conversation. I could hear it from the hallway."

Lydia chuckled softly. "We've been comparing notes..."

Barton took a seat in his usual armchair, the fatigue of the day beginning to settle in his bones. He offered to make another pot of tea, but both women declined, clearly still absorbed in their discussion. He leaned back, considering how much to share with them about the day's developments. On the one hand, the case was sensitive, and there were aspects he was still piecing together himself. On the other hand, both Lydia and Miranda had been close to Evelyn with a deep understanding of her and her work.

After a moment's hesitation, Barton decided to bring them into the loop. If they could offer clarity where he was struggling, it would be worth it. "I had an interesting day," he began, his tone reflective. "We've been re-evaluating the direction of the investigation, particularly regarding the *Vita Regis* manuscript."

Miranda's expression shifted to one of keen interest "Oh? What did you discover?"

Barton glanced at Lydia, who gave him an encouraging nod. "Well, after some thought, and thanks to a discussion I had with Lydia last night, I've started to consider the possibility that the *Vita Regis* might be a hoax. Something designed to distract us from the real motive behind Evelyn's murder."

Miranda didn't look entirely surprised, but she was thoughtful. "I've been wondering about that myself," she admitted. "There's something off about the whole thing. When Evelyn was alive, she never mentioned the *Vita Regis* to me by name, not in any of our conversations, not in any of her notes to which I had access, and Evelyn wasn't one to keep something so significant entirely to herself, especially when it came to research. She trusted me."

Barton nodded, appreciating her honesty. "That's exactly what's been bothering me since our conversation, Lyd. If the *Vita Regis* was as important as we've been led to believe, why isn't there more evidence of it in Evelyn's work before Edward Voss's abrupt departure? It seems like it only came into focus after he left, almost as if it was introduced into the story by someone else."

Lydia, who had been listening quietly, spoke up. "Miranda and I were just talking about that before you came in. Evelyn was secretive, yes, but she wasn't careless. The package of the *Vita Regis* papers that she left here was part of her research that she believed to be important. She did speak to a few people about it, remember your trip to Professor Lowman – he said she was focused on the manuscript, but the only hard evidence about the *Vita Regis* seems to come from Evelyn's papers and notebooks.

Barton rubbed his chin thoughtfully. "So do you now both believe that the *Vita Regis* might be a complete red herring that fooled Evelyn and our investigation?"

Miranda nodded. "Yes – and if that's the case, the *Vita Regis* could be a hoax used to obscure the real motive for Evelyn's murder, ones that have nothing to do with the manuscript itself."

Lydia chimed in. "What if the motive was purely personal? Jealousy, revenge or something else entirely? You have been so focused on the academic angle, Whip, but Evelyn's life was more than just her work. Voss might have had a personal vendetta or a grievance that had nothing to do with her work."

Barton leaned back in his chair, processing their words. It was yet another step away from the *Vita Regis*, one that may lead them down a completely different path. Also, if the *Vita*

Regis was just a story, it could be completely ignored.

"Miranda," Barton said after a moment, "you knew Evelyn well. Did she ever express concerns about Voss? Anything that might suggest a falling out or a deeper issue between them?"

Miranda looked down at her hands, which were clasped tightly in her lap. "There was such a gap between Voss leaving and me starting, he was rarely even mentioned. Evelyn was always careful with her words, but on the very rare occasions he mentioned him, she seemed…equally frustrated with herself as she was with Voss. He was brilliant, no doubt about that, but he had a way of pushing her buttons. He could be dismissive of her ideas, especially if they didn't align with his. There were also rumours that Voss was envious of Evelyn's success, that he felt overshadowed by her. Maybe it was just a case of unrequited love?"

Lydia added, "Jealousy can be a powerful motivator, especially in academic circles. If Voss felt threatened or slighted by Evelyn, he might have seen a hoax like *Vita Regis* as a way to regain some of the attention he felt he deserved."

Barton nodded slowly, piecing together the implications. "If Voss introduced the *Vita Regis* as a distraction, then the real motive could be something much more personal. Something rooted in his relationship, or lack of, with Evelyn."

Miranda's gaze was steady as she spoke. "I think we need to consider the possibility that Voss was involved in Evelyn's murder, not because of some grand academic conspiracy, but because of something much more human. The *Vita Regis* was his way of throwing the investigation off the scent or even retaliation."

The room fell silent as they considered this idea. Barton could feel they really were dealing with something far simpler than a murder motivated by academic rivalry. This was personal, deeply personal, and it had taken them this long to see it.

Miranda looked at him, her expression excited at being

a witness to the breakthrough in the case. "What's the next step?"

"Voss has already been arrested and bailed for assaulting his wife, and we will be questioning him further about Evelyn tomorrow," Barton replied. "But this time, we're not asking about the *Vita Regis* at all. We're asking about his relationship with Evelyn, about his feelings towards her, about what he was doing in the days leading up to and the night of her murder. We'll be looking for any cracks in his story, anything that suggests he's hiding something."

As the evening wore on, the three of them continued to discuss the case, bouncing ideas off each other and formulating a plan of action. By the time they said their goodbyes and Miranda left for the night, Barton felt more confident than he had in days. He and Lydia sat together on the sofa, Pip now awake and nestled between them, providing a comforting warmth.

"You really think you're onto something, don't you?" Lydia asked softly.

"I do," Barton replied. "We've been chasing the wrong lead all along, but now we're back on track."

Lydia lay her head on his shoulder, her hand resting gently on his. "I know you will, Whip." They sat in companionable silence for a while, the fire crackling softly in the background. As the night deepened and the house grew quiet, Barton closed his eyes, allowing himself a moment of peace. Tomorrow would bring new challenges, but for now, he was content to sit here with his wife and Pip.

Chapter 29

The following morning, Voss sat slumped in a chair in the interview room, having been picked up again for further questioning. His hands rested in his lap, fingers twitching slightly as though itching to take up a pen and paper, to start weaving another of his elaborate stories.

Barton and DS Jane Hughes, an officer with much training and experience in dealing with domestic abuse cases, sat opposite Voss. Barton started the official recording, announcing the date, time and location of the interview, as well as the names of those present.

After a short pause, Barton began, "Edward Voss," his voice steady, "you have been bailed after your arrest for the assault on Victoria Berger. I will now read you your rights once more. You do not have to say anything, but it may harm your defence if you do not mention when questioned something you later rely on in court. Anything you do say may be given in evidence."

Voss's only response was a thin, mirthless smile. "About time, Inspector, and for the record I decline a solicitor to be present, I certainly don't want the Berger's lap dog in his smart suit and smart car to be involved," he said quietly, as though the arrest were little more than a formality, a prelude to the greater performance he was eager to give.

"Mr Voss," Barton began, "we're here to discuss the assault on Victoria Berger. You've been arrested in connection with this incident, and we need to hear your account of what happened."

Voss leaned back in his chair, his expression bored and goaded. "What do you want to know, Inspector? You've already spoken to Victoria, haven't you? I'm sure she's painted me as the villain of the piece."

"We're interested in hearing your side of the story," Barton replied evenly. "Tell us what happened."

For a moment, Voss seemed to consider his words, then shrugged and spoke in a bored drawl as if explanation was beneath him and he was talking to a four-year-old. "Victoria and I argued. It happens in marriages, doesn't it? People argue, tempers flare. She said some things, I said some things. And yes, I hit her. I'm not proud of it, but there it is. I lost control."

"Why did you lose control, Edward?" Hughes asked, her tone gentle but probing. "What was the argument about?"

Voss's eyes flicked to Hughes, then back to Barton. "Oh, please, are you playing good cop, bad cop? I had thought better of you, Inspector." He paused. "It was about Evelyn Merton, of course. Everything's been about her lately, hasn't it? Victoria's been needling me about my connection to Evelyn ever since she died. I suppose she thought I was too close to her. But Victoria doesn't understand, she never understood what Evelyn and I shared."

"And what did you share with Dr Merton?" Barton pressed.

Voss's lips curled into a small, knowing smile. "Ah, Inspector, now that is the real question, isn't it? What did I share with Evelyn? More than Victoria could ever comprehend. Evelyn was a genius, a mind like no other. We were kindred spirits, she and I, bound by our love for the quest for knowledge, for discovery. But she was blind to what we could have had, blinded by her ambition, her own need for control. She underestimated me, and I couldn't tolerate that; it had to end."

Barton exchanged a glance with Hughes. They hadn't anticipated this; the shift from the assault charge to the deeper, more sinister subject of Voss's feelings towards Dr Merton had happened so quickly. Barton made a quick decision.

"Edward Voss, given what you have just said", Barton, his voice calm but firm, began, "I'm now re-cautioning you on suspicion of the murder of Dr Evelyn Merton. You do not have to say anything, but it may harm your defence if you do not mention when questioned something you later rely on in court. Anything you do say may be given in evidence. Do you understand?"

Voss's smile widened, a glint of satisfaction in his eyes. "I understand perfectly, Inspector. I have been expecting this for some time. I suppose this is where the real fun begins," while staring at Barton and Hughes with his cold, humourless smile.

The tension in the room had shifted. Voss's energy changed from detached to something almost euphoric, as though he had been an actor waiting for his moment in the spotlight after years of being an understudy. Barton could see it in his eyes, a twisted eagerness to unburden himself, not out of guilt, but out of a desire to flaunt his cleverness, to show just how thoroughly he believed he had outwitted them all.

"Tell us about your relationship with Dr Merton," Barton prompted, keeping his tone neutral.

Voss leaned forward, resting his elbows on the table, his fingers beneath his chin. "My relationship with Evelyn was... complicated. As I said, we were kindred spirits. I admired her mind, her intellect. But Evelyn was always so distant, always kept me at arm's length. She couldn't see what was right in front of her, that we were meant to be together, to work together. She rejected me, Inspector. Rejected my advances, my feelings. And that...that wounded me deeply."

Hughes interjected softly, "Is that why you wanted to ruin

her? Because she rejected you?"

Voss's gaze shifted to Hughes, his expression hardening to a sneer. It was becoming apparent that Miranda had been right – he really did have a problem with intelligent women in general. "It wasn't just about rejection. It was about power. Evelyn thought she was untouchable, that she could spurn me and continue with her life as though nothing had happened. But she underestimated me. She underestimated what I am capable of."

"And that's when you came up with the idea of the *Vita Regis*?" Barton asked, steering the conversation towards the heart of the matter.

Voss's eyes gleamed with a perverse pride. "Yes, the *Vita Regis*. A magnificent piece of fiction, if I do say so myself. You see, Inspector, I knew Evelyn would never fall for something as crude as blackmail or threats. She was too clever for that. But I also knew that her reputation was everything to her. It started as a prank, I began about a year before I left the University, planting the seeds of the idea of *Vita Regis*'s existence; small hints, whispers, documents that seemed to suggest it was real, always keeping my identity hidden. I could see she had completely fallen into an obsessive spiral, wanting to solve the puzzle of the *Vita Regis*. I had needed her to believe in it, to chase after it, to want to invest herself in proving its existence. Then, after I had to leave the University, I realised that my revenge could be completely unleashed."

Barton's voice remained steady, though his mind was racing as he pieced together the implications of Voss's confession. "So was your revenge to ruin her professional reputation using the *Vita Regis* hoax?"

Voss chuckled softly, a sound devoid of warmth. "Simple, really. Once Evelyn was fully invested in the *Vita Regis* and had published her paper on her findings, I would have leaked the truth, anonymously, of course. The academic community would have turned on her in an instant. Her credibility, her legacy, everything she had worked for, her reputation would have crumbled."

Hughes asked, "But why murder, Edward? Why not just expose her? Why go to such extremes?"

Voss's smile faded, replaced by a cold, calculating expression. "Because I realised that Evelyn was too strong, too resilient. Even if her reputation was tarnished, she would have found a way to recover. She would have fought back, and in the end, she might have won, and that would never do. No, the only way to truly defeat her was to ensure she could never recover her reputation. If she were silenced, this would have left her legacy as the academic who fell for the *Vita Regis* hoax. It has quite a good ring to it, doesn't it? The tabloids would love it: 'Don Done Down Drama' - quite the catchy headline."

Barton felt a chill run down his spine as Voss's words sank in. There was no remorse in his voice, no regret for the life he had taken. Only a chilling pride in the genius of his plan.

Barton took a risk, his voice tight with the effort to maintain his composure. "Tell us about the night of the murder. How did you do it?"

Voss leaned back in his chair, his eyes taking on a distant, almost dreamy quality as he recounted the events of that fateful night.

"I have nothing to lose by telling the story; my life is effectively ruined. It was surprisingly easy," he began. "You see, Evelyn was a woman of strict routine, so much so that you could almost set your watch by it. I knew that every Thursday evening she would go to the Chapter House to review documents, going over the details of her research. For many years, I had been planting clues and hints about the *Vita Regis,* weaving an impenetrable web; she would spend hours in the Chapter House trying to unravel the riddle from the fragments I had anonymously fed her. Sometimes I was in the Chapter House too. Just watching. But she never even recognised me."

Voss paused, as if savouring the memory. "That night I was in the Chapter House waiting for her, just as the Cathedral was closing; it was just the two of us, no one else in the room. I had everything prepared, a water bottle identical to hers with the poison mixed with water. She was completely absorbed by her documents; she didn't even notice when I walked past and swapped the bottles on the desk. I had watched her from the other side of the Chapter House so many times, I knew her routine inside out.

"What poison did you use?" Hughes asked, her voice barely above a whisper.

Voss smiled faintly. "Aconitine. Also known as monkshood or wolfsbane, something poetic about using a medieval herb, don't you think? It's a potent neurotoxin, causes paralysis and death within minutes if ingested in a sufficient quantity. I chose it because it's relatively rare and difficult to trace at autopsy, as it is absorbed and disappears from the average body within 60 hours after being taken."

"And then?" Barton prompted, his heart pounding as he imagined the scene Voss was describing.

Voss's voice took on a clinical tone, as if he were discussing a scientific experiment. "Evelyn didn't suspect a thing. She drank the water as she worked, and within minutes, she started to feel the effects. At first, it appeared that she was just tired, perhaps a little dizzy; she must have known something was wrong. She tried to speak, to ask me for help, but by then it was too late. The poison was doing its job."

Barton felt a surge of anger and revulsion, but he forced himself to remain calm to keep Voss talking. "What did you do next?"

"I watched…and waited," Voss replied, his voice devoid of emotion. "I waited until I was sure she was dead. I had adjusted the lock of the main door so that it would appear to be locked from the outside and pushed the door closed. Then, when I heard the nightwatchman's key in the lock, I knew I had plenty of time to arrange her body and the table in front of her, as if she had been working right up until the end. I wanted it to look natural, as if she had simply passed away while doing what she loved. Of course, I took her phone, her wallet and her university ID card to slow down identification, and swapped the water bottles back."

"And how did you ensure that the Chapter House door remained unlocked?" Barton asked, trying to connect the dots.

Voss's smile returned, smug and self-satisfied. "That was the easiest part, really. The Cathedral's medieval security system is outdated, to say the least. I've spent some time researching so I knew how to bypass the medieval lock mechanism on the Chapter House door from the inside. It's a simple matter of disabling the internal latch, something that can be done with a thin piece of metal or a credit card, for instance. I knew that the nightwatchman, a man of habit, wouldn't open the door to check the room once it was closed, and the sound of the key in the lock confirmed that I was right."

"And you stayed in the Chapter House overnight with Dr Merton's body?" Hughes asked, her voice filled with the horror of what she was hearing.

Voss nodded. "Yes. After I had finished my work arranging the scene, I found a quiet corner near one of the alcoves and observed the tableau I had created. I knew the Cathedral would be opened early the next morning for the first services in one of the side chapels, and I could simply slip into the cloisters and leave with the congregation. No one would suspect a thing. I had even taken the trouble to occasionally join the congregation for the early service for a month or so before, so I wasn't seen as a stranger when I joined them."

Barton felt a wave of nausea as Voss finished his story, the full extent of the man's cold-bloodedness sinking in. But he couldn't afford to let his emotions get the better of him, not yet.

"We found a small note in her pocket that said, 'The past

is a shadow that shapes the present' Was that from you or a favourite quote of Dr Merton?"

"My dear Barton, it was my last message to her and my first to you. Over the years, I have left many messages for her to find. Just to mess with her head, keep her guessing, make her feel insecure, allow self-doubt to grow. Self-doubt is a terrible affliction for an academic; it grows and rots inside you. This was an inconsequential literary flourish designed purely to distract." Voss said with a sneer.

"The arson at Dr Merton's cottage," Barton said, steering the conversation to the final piece of the puzzle. "Why did you burn it down?"

Voss's expression darkened, his earlier smugness replaced by a flicker of anger. "Contrary to the University's story that they had kept her address secret, I had had it since the day she moved in. I had been watching her to assess her stress and to see how I could add to it. I had set up a couple of small cameras around the cottage. I didn't want to have to keep going over to Pinhoe, such a drab little village. So, I knew you had been to the cottage and that you would be getting too close, Inspector. I didn't want to risk you finding any records that gave an alternative story to the ones I had planted in her office. The cottage had to be a dead end, a place where no contrary story could be found. I guessed you may find something in her forest of papers. I knew I had to act quickly. The fire was a last resort, a way to destroy any remaining evidence of her research into the *Vita Regis*, if she had suspicions about it being a hoax and anything that could possibly link me to Evelyn."

"You thought you could outsmart us, but you didn't know or had missed was we had already taken some things away," Barton said quietly, his eyes fixed on Voss. "But in the end, you made mistakes, mistakes that led us right to you."

Voss sneered, his earlier composure beginning to crack. "You got lucky, Inspector. That's all. If it hadn't been for a few unfortunate coincidences, you'd still be chasing ghosts.

One thing I hadn't anticipated was that her current assistant would be quite so smart. I met her, you know, at a café, at her request; she had made some connections that I hadn't anticipated, but she also revealed her hand so I could adjust my plan accordingly. She had no idea she had helped me when she thought she was helping with the investigation. She seemed so inconsequential, so plodding, I thought she was just some bimbo, biding her time before she married and had kids," he sneered.

Barton leaned forward, his voice low and filled with quiet intensity. "You're wrong, Edward. It wasn't luck that brought us here. It was your arrogance, your belief that you could manipulate everyone around you without consequence. You underestimated Evelyn, Miranda, and you underestimated us. And now, you'll pay the price for what you've done."

Voss glared at Barton, his hands clenching into fists and pounding them on the table. But there was no denying the truth of Barton's words. The game was over, and Voss had lost.

The interview concluded with Barton formally charging Edward Voss with the murder of Dr Evelyn Merton. Voss's story seemed to hang heavily in the air as the recording device was switched off, and Voss was led away to his cell, his smugness finally giving way to the realisation of what lay ahead.

As Barton and Hughes watched Voss being taken into custody, they felt a mix of emotions: primarily relief that they had finally caught the killer, revulsion at his callous and calculated planning of the murder and sorrow for the life that had been lost. Neither of them had ever come across anyone quite like Voss before, and they hoped they wouldn't ever again.

The case was over, apart from the inevitable paperwork and collation of evidence, but with Voss's confession in hand, they could now compile all of their reports into a case and hand them on to the Crown Prosecution Service to bring Voss to court. Evelyn Merton's killer would finally be brought to justice.

Chapter 30

The Sunday sun hung low in the sky, casting a golden glow over Topsham as Barton, Lydia, Miranda, Brooks and his partner Amelia strolled along the narrow streets. The afternoon was warm, with just the faintest whisper of an autumn breeze coming off the river, carrying with it the scent of the sea. It was the kind of late summer day that seemed to stretch on endlessly, inviting long walks and deep conversations.

They had just finished a hearty lunch at The Passage, a pub with a very long history and many stories to tell. The food had been as good as ever, a classic Sunday roast with all the trimmings, roast beef, Yorkshire pudding, crispy roast potatoes, and rich gravy had left everyone feeling pleasantly replete. Sitting at a table on the river's edge never got old, and now that they were moving into autumn, the opportunities for outside dining would be less frequent until next spring. Pip, of course, had been the lucky recipient of a few choice scraps, which he had gobbled down with enthusiasm, his tail wagging vigorously. Miranda had taken a particular liking to Pip, scratching his ears and feeding him morsels under the table. Pip, in return, had decided that Miranda was now his third favourite person after Barton and Lydia.

As they started their walk, the group naturally fell into pairs and trios, conversations flowing and shifting as they strolled along the river towards the boardwalk heading to

Exmouth. The water sparkled in the afternoon light, and the boats moored along the river bobbed gently with the tide; soon they would be lifted out of the river until the next sailing season, for Barton, the real marker point in the change of seasons. It was a picture-perfect day in Topsham, the kind of day that made Barton appreciate the slower pace of life in Devon.

Pip trotted along beside them, his nose twitching as he sniffed the air, eyes bright and alert for any more potential snacks or interesting smells. Pip had become quite the connoisseur of Sunday walks, and today, with a belly full of scraps, he was in especially high spirits, bounding between the groups, greeting each as if they had not seen each other for years and then, after being acknowledged, charging off to another group.

Brooks and Barton found themselves walking together at the front of the party. Brooks was still mulling over the events of the past week, particularly the chilling confession of Edward Voss. His sharp mind was constantly at work, and though the case had been solved, he couldn't help but go over the details again in his head.

"That confession," Saxon began, his voice low, almost as if he were reluctant to break the tranquillity of the afternoon. "It was unlike anything I've ever heard. The way Voss spoke, so detached, so cold. It's hard to believe someone could do something so monstrous and then talk about it as if it were no more than a walk to the corner shop."

Barton nodded, his eyes on the path ahead. "I've seen my share of killers, Saxon, but Voss... he's different. It's not just that he committed the murder; it's the way he planned it, the way he took pride in outsmarting everyone. There's a cruelty in that, a need to show his superiority – and sitting with the body all night to then make his escape in the congregation, that is cold."

Saxon looked thoughtful. "And yet, he was brought

down by his arrogance. He completely believed in his own brilliance, making him invulnerable, and that's what led to his downfall in the end."

Barton couldn't help but smile at that. "Arrogance has a way of blinding people to their inadequacies. Voss thought he could control everything, but in the end, he couldn't even control himself."

They walked in silence for a few moments, each lost in their thoughts, the sound of their footsteps blending with the gentle lapping of the river against the shore.

Behind them, Lydia and Miranda were deep in conversation, their voices a quiet murmur carried on the breeze. Lydia had been intrigued by Miranda's academic background, and they had quickly found common ground in their shared love of research and discovery.

"I've been thinking," Lydia said, glancing at Miranda. "What you said the other day, about the *Vita Regis*. You were right to doubt it. The more I think about it, the more I see how easily we can be misled when we're searching for something we desperately want to be true."

Miranda nodded, her expression serious. "It's a powerful lesson, isn't it? Evelyn was so brilliant, but even she was vulnerable to deception. Voss knew exactly how to manipulate her, and he almost succeeded in destroying her reputation. If we hadn't uncovered the truth…"

"We will learn from this," Lydia interrupted, her voice firm. "Evelyn's death won't be in vain. I want to continue her work, not on the *Vita Regis*, but on the real history she had been uncovering. I am going to apply for a research role at the University and I want to work with you, Miranda. We could do great things together."

Miranda smiled, a warm, genuine smile that softened her often intense expression. "I'd like that, Lydia. I think we could make a formidable team."

Lydia returned the smile, feeling a sense of camaraderie

that had grown over the past few days. She hadn't expected to find a friend in Miranda, but now she couldn't imagine not having her by her side. She tucked her arm through Miranda's as they continued to walk.

A little further back, Amelia was walking with Pip at her side. She watched as the retriever ambled back and forth, sniffing at the grass, his enthusiasm for life contagious. Amelia had only recently moved to Devon with Saxon, and the culture shock of leaving Peckham in Southeast London for the slower, quieter life in the countryside had been significant.

"This place is so different from London," Amelia said, catching up with Lydia and Miranda. The blend of Peckham and Nigerian accent was distinctive, a reminder of the world she had left behind. "Everything's so quiet, so…slow. I'm not sure I'll ever get used to it."

Lydia chuckled softly. "It takes time, but once you do, you may find you don't want to leave. There's a peace here that's hard to find anywhere else. And there's always something happening beneath the surface. You just have to know where to look."

Amelia nodded, her eyes drifting out over the river. "Saxon loves it here. He's always been drawn to quiet places like this; I suppose it suits him. As a card-carrying tech nerd, he just needs his screen, peace, a decent internet connection and a problem to solve. I just…I miss the energy and noise of the city, you know?"

Miranda smiled at Amelia. "I understand. It's an adjustment, moving to a place like this. We'll have to go out together one night, and I'll show you another side of the city you probably haven't found yet. We'll make a proper night of it." They quickly shared each other's mobile numbers and promised to call soon.

Amelia looked thoughtful. "That would be great, going out with someone my age would be a breath of fresh air. I am the youngest in the department by about 50 years." She laughed. "I guess I just need to find my own rhythm here. I am enjoying the bio-sciences department at the University, although they do treat me like a rare specimen. Maybe it's just my bright clothes and head scarves!" she smiled a smile that lit up her face and moved to rejoin Brooks.

Barton joined Lydia and Miranda as they reached a particularly scenic stretch of the path, where the river widened and the view opened up to the distant hills on the other side of the estuary. "You two seem to have hit it off," he remarked, his tone light.

Lydia nodded. "We have. And we've decided to work together on some research. There's a lot of untapped potential in Evelyn's work, even without the *Vita Regis*."

Barton smiled. "I'm glad to hear that. Evelyn's legacy deserves to be preserved by people who truly understand and respect it."

Miranda added, "And we'll be careful not to let anyone else manipulate us. We've seen what can happen when someone like Voss gets involved."

Barton nodded gravely "Voss was a reminder of how dangerous knowledge can be when it's wielded by the wrong person. He was brilliant in his own way, but that brilliance was twisted by his obsession with control, with proving himself superior."

Lydia looked at her husband, her expression thoughtful. "It's frightening. How someone can take something as pure as the pursuit of knowledge and turn it into something dark, something deadly, with no ability to see that anything he had done was wrong…a true narcissist"

Miranda added quietly, "And Evelyn paid with her life."

A silence fell over the group as they walked, each lost in their thoughts. The events of the past weeks had left a mark on all of them, a reminder of the fine line between brilliance and madness, between the pursuit of truth and the descent into darkness.

Pip, sensing the change in mood, trotted back to Barton's side, looking up at him with bright, curious eyes. Barton reached down to scratch behind his dog's ears, grateful for the simple comfort of his loyal companion.

As they reached the end of the boardwalk and the path began to wind towards Lympstone, the group slowly came back together, the conversations becoming lighter, more focused on the present rather than the past.

"Pip seems to have taken quite a liking to Miranda," Amelia observed with a smile. "Lydia says he's usually very particular about people."

Barton chuckled. "Pip has good instincts. He can tell when someone's worth trusting."

Miranda laughed softly. "I'm honoured to have Pip's approval."

Saxon, who had been watching Pip with a mixture of amusement and puzzlement, shook his head. "I still don't quite get him. Dogs are so…unpredictable. But I suppose that's part of their charm."

Lydia smiled. "Pip's not just a dog, Saxon. He's family."

Pip, seemingly understanding that he was the subject of the conversation, barked once, his tail wagging vigorously. The group laughed, the tension of the earlier conversation finally lifting as they continued their walk.

As they approached the village of Lympstone, the sun began to dip lower over the hills, casting long shadows across the path. The air was cooler now, and the first hints of evening were beginning to settle in.

The village itself was picturesque, with its cottages and narrow lanes, and the group paused for a moment to take in the view. It was the kind of place that seemed untouched by time, where life moved at the same pace as the river, unhurried and peaceful.

As they stood there, looking out over the river and the distant hills, Barton felt a deep sense of contentment. The case had been difficult, but it had also brought them all closer together, forged bonds of new friendships that he knew would endure long after the case was closed.

Lydia and Miranda were talking softly about their plans for the future, their voices filled with enthusiasm and a shared sense of purpose. Saxon and Amelia stood a little apart from the rest of the group, Saxon's arm around Amelia's shoulders as they looked out over the water. Pip sat at Barton's feet, his head resting on Barton's leg, his eyes half-closed in contentment.

Barton looked at the people around him with a feeling of intense gratitude. They had been through a lot together.

As they turned to make their way back towards Topsham, Barton knew that this was just the beginning of something new. Pip trotted ahead, his tail wagging as if to lead the way home, and the group followed, their steps lighter now, their hearts a little warmer.

The walk back was filled with laughter and conversation, the earlier darkness of their discussion about Voss's confession put aside for now. They talked about the future, about their plans and hopes, and as the evening settled in, there was a sense of closure and of new beginnings.

As they reached the outskirts of Topsham, the lights of the town were starting to twinkle. Barton felt a sense of peace. Walking together into the gathering dusk, Barton knew that he was with friends; Pip, as if sensing Barton's thoughts, looked up at him and barked once, a sound of pure joy. Barton smiled, reaching down to pat his head.

"Yes, Pip," he said softly. "We did well. We all did.

And with that, they walked on, into the night, the river whispering its secrets to the stars above.

www.ingramcontent.com/pod-product-compliance
Lightning Source LLC
Chambersburg PA
CBHW061218170626
46809CB00007B/2521